WAITING

Q. Kelly

D1528085

Acknowledgements

Melanie, my wife, deserves a medal for her support and patience.

Also, special thanks to Rina Wojcik and to the others who preferred to not be named. All of you helped me very much, and you all rock.

Q.Kelly on the Web:

http://qkelly.blogspot.com
http://qkelly.wordpress.com

I would love to hear from you!
Email me at yllek_q@yahoo.com

Ride the Rainbow Books
www.ridetherainbowbooks.com

This book is a work of fiction. Any resemblance
to actual persons living or dead or actual events
is purely coincidental.

No part of this book may be reproduced
without the permission of the author.

"Waiting" Copyright © 2010 by Q. Kelly

Chapter 1

Caris sighed, trying not to say her wife's name, even if it was just in her mind. But she could not help it. *Dale. Dale. Where are you? There's no excuse. It's 10 a.m.!*

Their son was five hours old, and the labor had lasted ten hours. So why was Dale not at the hospital yet? Yeah, she and Caris had fought. And yeah, Caris had accused Dale of behavior bordering on emotional abuse — a completely justified accusation. Caris had threatened separation.

But this was a baby, their baby. Maybe Caris was not worth more to Dale than the plastic crap at Dollar General, but the baby was. Dale getting a hotel room had nothing to do with the baby. So why was she not at the hospital yet? Caris and her mother, Phyllis Zinn, had left so many messages on Dale's voice mail that it was full. The front desk clerks at the Holiday Inn probably hated Phyllis's raspy ex-smoker's voice. No one at the law firm had seen or heard from Dale.

Maybe because the baby had come a couple of weeks early, it had not entered Dale's mind that all the messages were about the arrival of their son. Better to believe that than other things.

Caris reached for the picture a nurse had snapped of her and the baby. "For Dale," the nurse had said with a sympathetic smile. Caris hardly recognized herself. She usually had a perfect part in the middle of her head for the blond hair down to her waist. Not so in the picture. From the neck up, Caris looked like she was on the set of a horror movie, maybe having just fled Freddy or Jason. Her eyes were manic, her hair was in a careless ponytail, red splotched her cheeks, and sweat shone on her forehead, her cheeks and her chin. She looked forty-five, not thirty, and her body was a new mother's funhouse-mirror mixture of willowy and bulge. The photo did not show one of her prettier moments, but her son was worth it. If only she could focus on him and not on where his other mother was.

"You're a good boy, good boy, yes, you are." Phyllis cuddled the baby and rocked him. Caris's mother was nearing sixty, but years of alcohol abuse, cigarette abuse, and sun worship had accelerated her aging. She was rail thin and had a fondness for gaudy jewelry. Today's necklace was centered around a plastic rhinoceros, courtesy of Dale. Dale knew the way to Phyllis's heart.

Phyllis met Caris's eyes. "She'll come." Like mother, like daughter. They would not say Dale's name to each other, not yet. They would keep it unspoken that something could be gravely wrong.

But things already *were* gravely wrong.

"What the hell," Caris muttered. Time to say the name out loud. "Dale doesn't love me, Mom. Not anymore. We're done. It's too exhausting."

Phyllis raised a disapproving eyebrow. "You'll work it out, whatever it is."

Caris forced a deep breath. Dale, not Phyllis, should have been the one with Caris when the baby was born. Dale, of all people, was supposed to be different. She was older, fifty-six. She had salt and pepper hair and lines of wisdom crinkling her eyes. She admitted readily that she had used to sleep around but had not for years. She was done sowing oats. Wrong? Caris was not sure what to think anymore. If nothing had happened to Dale, that meant she was acting like a child, pouting and not coming to the hospital to be with her wife and new baby.

"There must be an explanation," Phyllis said.

Caris did not answer. No point doing so. Phyllis knew nothing about romantic relationships. She was a butterfly, a flitter. Kind of like Lena, Dale's daughter from her previous marriage to a gay man. However, Lena was in a relationship now, if on and off seemingly every other week for one year counted as a relationship.

In any case, Dale had not slept in the same bed as her for the past three weeks and refused to say why. Dale barely spoke to Caris, except to criticize her or to inquire after the pregnancy. The freeze-out had begun about six months ago with no apparent cause. Was there another woman? Dale had said no.

Dale got drunk and ran away with the other woman, the mistress.
Dale's been in a car crash.
Dale's ignoring me because she thinks I'm tiresome. Because I have crazy hormones.
Dale's pulling a gigantic April Fool's joke on me.
How long should I wait before calling the police?
I'm going to kill her.

The door opened. "Hello!" came two excited voices and a trail of blue balloons. Dale's parents. George and Shirley had driven the eight hours from Rhode Island to Northern Virginia, to the Inova Fairfax Hospital.

"Hey!" Caris smiled. Dale's parents were good people, and she was glad to see them. Sometimes she had a hard time believing Shirley and George were eighty-two years old, because they looked more alive, more energetic, than leathery Phyllis.

Shirley darted for the blue bundle in Phyllis's lap. "He's beautiful," Shirley exclaimed, awe filling her voice.

"He's the spitting image of Dale," Phyllis agreed, letting Shirley take him. The donor from the sperm bank had done his job, and then some.

Shirley grinned at Caris. "He has your beautiful blue eyes."

Thank goodness he doesn't have George's ears. George was a beanpole with high, floppy ears. Shirley was her husband's opposite, plump and barely topping five feet tall. Her hair was mostly white, but a few black skunk-like streaks survived. She and Dale both had brown eyes, but Shirley's tended toward friendliness, while Dale's were almost always intense. No gaudy jewelry for Shirley; she would not be caught dead with a plastic rhino on her chest. Her necklace was pearl, simple and understated. She was from old Providence family money and had married George, a poor boy from the wrong side of the tracks.

"What's his name?" George asked.

"I haven't decided." Caris liked the name Milo for a boy; Dale liked the name Donovan. The baby was one of the few subjects Dale talked about with her in more than one-sentence or two-sentence replies. They had been discussing a compromise: Milo Donovan Ismay or Donovan Milo Ismay.

"I called the hotel right before we arrived," George said. "Seems like Dale hasn't been back to the room." He did not ask why Dale and Caris had been fighting, although the curious lilt of his voice gave his interest away.

"Did we miss Lena?" Shirley asked.

Caris stifled a snort. Dale not being at the hospital was unsettling. Lena's absence, on the other hand, was not unusual. Caris and Lena were not close. Lena's choice, not hers. Probably the curse of a same-age stepdaughter. Well, mostly same-age stepdaughter. Right now, Lena was twenty-nine, but four months out of the year, they were the same age.

Caris could not resist Shirley's beaming, expectant face. Shirley wanted good news, and by golly, she would get good news. "Lena's coming," Caris murmured. "She's out searching for Dale." Lena had not answered her cellphone either, but Caris would give her the benefit of the doubt. *Be a good stepmother. The baby will need his big sister. Especially if I'm going to be his only mother.*

*****

Caris's best friend, Jennifer, and her husband, Oliver, stopped by and threatened to kidnap the baby because he was too adorable for words. Jennifer was one of the most open-minded people Caris knew. They had been friends since they were in diapers, and Jennifer was a big reason

Caris had come through the past few months relatively sane.

And then there was Lena, her brown hair pulled back in a ponytail, but without its usual efficiency. Lena liked her hair tight and hated loose strands. This ponytail was a mess, reminding Caris of her own *Nightmare on Elm Street* hair in the picture with the baby.

"Door was open," Lena mumbled. Her voice was slightly off, and if this were just another day, Caris would not have picked up on the tremor in her words. Caris looked closer at Lena, noticing dirt and grease streaking her hair. The lower half of her left arm was in a fresh cast.

"Lena!" Shirley passed the baby off to George. She placed a delicate hand on the cast and tried to look into Lena's avoiding eyes. "Your arm! What happened?"

Lena muttered something, Caris had no idea what, probably a little platitude to tide her grandparents over. Her eyes were white. Clear. Unmarred from crying. Largely uncommunicative, yes, par for the course when Lena was around Caris. The key was, Lena had not been crying. Everything was okay with her mother. Had to be, or she would be different.

Not really.

Caris's stomach became a lump of clay. Dale's daughter had come out of whatever happened with a broken arm. Dale had come out without her life. *She's dead. Dead. And the last time we saw each other, we were angry.* Caris's last words to her had been: "Fine. Run away! You know what that tells me? That you're guilty. You're hiding another woman! Is she waiting for you at the hotel?"

Lena shuffled over to Caris's area of the room, and Shirley took the baby back from George. "Look. Isn't he precious? Your little brother."

Lena managed a look and a tight-lipped smile. At least she was trying.

"Hey Caris," Lena said. She ran her right hand over her cheek, in what Caris recognized as a nervous habit and sometimes, a stalling tactic.

"Hello, Lena. Are you okay?"

A quick nod, hooded gaze. "Fine. Yeah."

Caris let the lie linger a long moment. Finally, she broke the silence but still was not ready to hear that her wife was dead. "Your eyes are brown right now."

Lena blinked. "What?"

"Sometimes they're brown. Green other times. But rarely both at the same time."

Lena frowned. "My eyes are brown. Period."

"They're hazel," Shirley put in. She held the baby in the crook of one arm and used her other hand to lift Lena's chin. "Yep. Beautiful hazel, just like your father's."

"Grandma, they're brown."

Shirley chuckled and summoned George for his opinion.

How's that for a stalling tactic.

Hard to believe sometimes that Dale and Lena were mother and daughter. While Dale was finicky and fussy about her appearance, keeping her short hair spiked and gelled and her business suits vibrant and crisp, Lena was all about jeans, T-shirts and comfort. Lena did have one skirt, dark green. She'd had the skirt for years, and as far as Caris knew, the skirt was the sole one Lena owned. It was so worn in and comfortable that Lena treated it as if it were another pair of jeans. Forget about dresses.

Dale was flat-chested, with parallel hips, while Lena had curves and enough cleavage to fill out a dress. Lena was soft and lovely in a way that Dale, with her sharp lines, intensity and drive, was not. They were both toned, however. Both jogged and worked out, although the middle-age battle of the bulge had a thirty-pound advantage on Dale.

Dale liked the more material aspects of life, while Lena did not care about money or status. She had gotten her bachelor's degree in art history, and a month after graduation, decided art history was not for her. She spent the next three years backpacking around Europe and "finding herself." Much to Dale's relief, Lena was back in school, working toward a master's in business administration. Lena was also working full time as a bartender. She refused financial support from Dale for graduate school.

"Did you find your mother?" Jennifer asked.

"Mom is…" Lena glanced toward the doorway. As if on cue, a policeman and an unfamiliar doctor appeared.

The fight flashed before Caris's eyes again. Dale's scowling. Dale's biting voice. Dale's squint. *I'm about to find out my wife is dead. Think of something good about us.* Dale whisking her away on a picnic. *See. We used to have good moments. A decent marriage.* More nice moments poured out: skiing at Snowshoe, getting lost in Paris on their honeymoon. Where and why had their marriage gone wrong?

Lena sank onto the bed and met Caris's eyes. That was how Caris knew for sure that something was wrong. Nothing hostile was in Lena's gaze. Just sorrow. Pity.

We're on the same side now, her eyes said.

Lena looked up at her grandparents. "Please give us a minute."

"No," Shirley said, choking on the word. "I'm staying right here. What's happened with your mother?"

"Please give us a minute, then I'll explain."

"I am staying right here. She's my daughter!"

"All right," Lena whispered. "Mom's been in an accident."

"What kind of accident?" Shirley asked.

"Car accident." Lena returned her focus to Caris. Took Caris's hands in hers. Lena's cast was sandpaper rough, but her skin was warm. Alive.

Caris's flesh prickled. "You're touching me." Lena and Caris had known each other four years, Caris had been her stepmother for three and a half years, and Lena had rarely deigned to touch her. When Lena did, it was for a quick handshake, or in stiff acceptance of a hug. Now here Lena was, touching Caris to *comfort* her.

Lena lowered her eyes, and Caris became even more conscious of Lena's hands on hers. Of Lena's heated, smooth skin. Feeling a new woman's warmth after months of being frozen out was nice.

Got Caris's mind off her dead wife, at any rate.

"Should I let go?" Lena asked. Her eyes were still brown, but now they had gold flecks, too. Must be the lighting.

Pretty eyes. Beautiful, alive eyes. *Please don't tell me your mother is dead.*

Lena let go.

Caris missed her contact immediately but did not reach out. A couple of messages, both in thin green Sharpie, were scrawled on Lena's cast.

Heal quickly! – Gino

Plenty of fish in the sea – Mom

Dale's message stopped Caris cold. *She's alive. She's okay.*

"What?" Lena synced her gaze with Caris's. "No, no, that…oh, geez."

Caris barked a brittle laugh.

"Listen," Lena said earnestly, and Caris caught a whiff of minty gum. In that moment, Lena was unbearably lovely, with her pale face, dirty hair and pained brown-gold eyes. "Listen to me. Mom's alive, but…"

Lena continued speaking, and Caris escaped to a dark place in the recesses of her mind. Words filtered through, anyway: *Almond's bar…crash truck thirty-five miles per hour, surgery…might not…driver's okay…but she has to, she will because of the baby, ribs, arms, legs, brain trauma…*

Caris realized just how many things could happen in sixty seconds. Eating a candy bar. Texting someone. Making a phone call. Going to the bathroom. Orgasm. Crashing your car. Devastating a family's life.

*****

Lena told her stepmother what needed to be said. She was faintly aware of her grandparents, and of Jennifer and Oliver, hovering at her side, of their sharp inhalations. No whimper from Caris, though. Just wide, unbelieving blue eyes. Thank God Caris was not crying. Her grandmother crying, okay, she could handle that. But not her mother. Not her stepmother.

"Your arm," Caris said. "What happened?"

"Did you hear me? Mom is—"

"I heard you. Your arm, what happened?"

"It's her wrist," Shirley said. "She fell." That was what Lena had mumbled to her grandparents: *I fell, you know how I'm clumsy…*

"Fell where?" Caris asked.

"My place."

"How?"

"Mom is—"

"Yes, I heard. How did you fall?"

"Tripped on a shoelace while I was running down the steps."

"Why?"

Lena snorted. "For the hell of it. A lark, eh?"

Caris narrowed her eyes. "Plenty of fish in the sea. Something happen with Caroline?"

"Mom is fighting for her life, and you're asking about Caroline?"

Caris's chin trembled. Maybe tears coming now. "I heard. Maybe I don't want to think about it."

You're a shit, Lena. She rose from the bed and waved the policeman and her mother's surgeon in. She let her grandmother hold Caris and imagined she had told the truth: *Well, Caroline and I were at my place. She was drunk out of her mind. She accused me of being in love with you. I denied it, walked out of the apartment to the staircase, Caroline tried to block me from leaving, we struggled, and I ended up kerplunking down the steps.*

Yeah. That would not go over so hot.

Chapter 2

Caris had to pee but kept putting it off. One nasty secret she had not learned until after the birth: doctors told you to lay off the toilet paper. She had a little squirt bottle to help clean herself up but did not see the point. She needed a hose. She was a gush of blood when she peed. The blood reached her thighs, calves, ankles. Caris wanted her body from nine months ago back. She hated her gargantuan vaginal lips, the stretch marks, the sore breasts.

Molly, the nurse who snapped the Friday the 13th picture, patted a wheelchair. "Pee before we go. You have your squirt bottle?" That was all the nurses asked. Squirt bottle, squirt bottle, squirt bottle. The world would end if she did not have a goddamn squirt bottle.

"I can wait."

"Go to the bathroom."

Caris sucked it up and peed. And bled.

Afterward, Molly patted the wheelchair again. "Let's go."

"Can't you forget hospital policy and let me walk?"

"Afraid not."

Caris sighed and got into the wheelchair. Ten a.m. had turned into four p.m. Time to visit Dale.

Caris ignored the inhuman mass and humming of machines and tubes as best as she could. She stared at the spider web of thick, dark stitches marring Dale's scalp. What kind of spider lived there? Tarantula, black widow? Definitely the kind that could kill. What did they eat? Flies, moths, ladybugs. Spiders were arachnids, right? Kind of like insects but with eight legs. Caris remembered her and Jennifer, both five years old, watching as Jennifer's tarantula, Freckles, ate Caris's pet baby mouse, Melanie. She had nightmares for a week. The tarantula had towered above the mouse, and Caris had felt something in her groin, fear, terror, something almost sexual, something *bad*, she knew. The tarantula lowered its mouth toward the mouse's head. Caris watched, terrified and fascinated, as the mouse *squee squee oh God help me squee* and then convulsed and was gone.

This mess was her wife. Dale's head was bare, shaved to let the stitches breathe. Doctors said she probably would not live through the night. They had no idea how she had made it this far already.

Caris held up the picture of her and the baby. "Donovan Milo Ismay," she whispered. "You win."

She recalled enough from Lena's mumblings and the haze of conversations with the police and Dale's surgeons to piece together how the accident happened. Yesterday, Lena had broken her wrist, called Dale to take her to the hospital, and afterward, they went to Almond's, a bar. Not the one where Lena worked, which made sense. Why go to the place you work when you're off duty? They had talked a while, and then Dale drove away in her Cadillac. Dale was returning to the hospital to be with her, Caris. Dale stopped at the Almond's parking lot exit, looked left, looked right, forgot to look left again, and pulled out in front of an eighteen-wheeler bearing down on her.

The eighteen-wheeler swerving, but not enough, plowing into Dale. The sickening, slow mashing of metal on metal, of Goliath pummeling David, hollering in victory.

The end of Dale, if not literally, then most likely for all practical purposes.

Caris felt a hand cover hers. "You okay, sweetie? You ready to go back to your room?"

Caris shook off Jennifer's touch. "I need to stay."

Phyllis this time: "You need to rest."

"I'm staying as long as I like. My wife will be dead the next time I see her."

*****

Shirley was in Dale's room, reading Dale a story, when Lena tiptoed in about midnight. "Hey, Grandma. Agatha Christie?" Agatha Christie was Dale's favorite author. Shirley's, too.

"Mmm. The *Seven Dials Mystery*. Novella. Want me to see about a cot for you, too?"

"I'm not staying. Just checking in on Mom." Lena sat in a chair, closed her eyes, and listened to the lift and fall of her grandmother's voice. *MacDonald looked upon her, and she blushed. She was made to feel that she had taken an unpardonable liberty...*

Unpardonable liberty. Interesting phrase. Lena liked it. She had taken two unpardonable liberties. First, lying to the nurse and doctor about being alone and tripping down the steps. The second unpardonable liberty: not turning over the note once she'd found it. Thank God the truck driver was okay, save for a few deep bruises.

"Grandma?" Lena asked.

Shirley glanced up. "Mmm?"

Lena's throat squeezed. "Mom never had a single speeding ticket or wreck. The accident doesn't make sense."

Shirley furrowed her brows. "What are you saying?"

"Maybe it wasn't an accident."

"Of course it was. Your mother wasn't thinking. She was in a hurry to be with Caris."

No, she wasn't. Mom looked left one last time. I saw it.

Shirley gave Lena a smile and returned to the story.

Lena fished the letter out of her Nintendo tote bag. The ER waiting room had been hell. The seconds were molasses, and Lena's mind was going crazy with thoughts. She'd read the letter maybe a hundred times. Probably had it memorized, but she felt the same nauseating dread every time she read it. Dale must have sneaked the letter into the tote bag while Lena was in the bathroom.

Lena,

I love you. I know I have not been a good mother. You deserve more. I look at you sometimes and I think: "Wow. This is my child. How did I get so lucky?" You're beautiful, strong, passionate, determined. You're very much like your father.

I've been thinking about you a lot these past few months as we've gotten closer and as I prepared to have another child. I hope someday you change your mind about wanting kids. You will be a fantastic mother. If you're afraid you will repeat my mistakes with your children, stop being afraid right now. You have learned from my mistakes and are the better for them.

You were, and are, magic in my life. Please always know that.

I wish three things for you. Happiness. Love. Laughter. Don't make the same mistakes I have when it comes to love.

I was thinking about Candy the other day. Candy Reese. Remember how I used to call her Reese Cup? I was also thinking about Melissa, and Joan, and Carmela. You know my sins, so I won't list them here. If you happen to see them again, though, please tell them I really did love them.

Please look after your little brother or sister after I'm gone. Please love that child the best you can, and please tell him or her I was a good person.

I love you,
Mom

Why hadn't she contacted the police about the note? Shock, maybe. That this couldn't really be happening. That her mother had left a suicide note. But her mother couldn't have known the truck would show up when it did. No matter. If not the truck, then something else.

Interesting that her mother had not mentioned Nakeem Joseph and Aron Michelle in the note. Maybe not so interesting, actually. It was likely that Dale did not think about them anymore. Or perhaps Dale liked to pretend Lena might not think about them anymore. Nakeem Joseph and Aron Michelle popped up in Lena's mind and in her heart at the most random times, like when she was serving a customer wine or when one of her professors was setting up a PowerPoint presentation.

Nakeem Joseph.

Aron Michelle.

She could call them "the twins." Their parents probably did. But they were two separate people with two separate, equally cool names. Nakeem Joseph and Aron Michelle was what she called them. Significant, nice names.

Anyway, so what was going through her mother's mind while she was waiting to pull out in the street? Maybe she had decided not to do it. She'd decided she wanted to live, but looked left one last time, saw a truck, and something, something, took over. She did it even as her body, her brain, were shouting: "No! No!"

Or maybe it was a cry for help. Daelyn Ismay was a planner. If she wanted to end her life, she would damn well end it the right way. She would leave nothing up to chance. For example, she would jump off a bridge.

Cry for help. That's what it has to be.

"Sweetie?" Shirley's voice jarred Lena out of her reverie. "I'm going to bed."

Lena kissed her grandmother goodbye. "Sleep well."

She made her way home. Driving with a cast was not too bad as long as she took turns slowly and carefully. She flopped onto her bed. She felt like a cardboard cutout. Princess Diana, next to the office nook across the bedroom, had a friend. Lena had bought the Diana cutout for $20 two years after the royal's death. She was not sure why. Diana's death had touched her, sure, but she did not lose herself in the wall to wall coverage. Did not stay up to watch the funeral.

Cardboard Diana's hair was short. No tiara, but she wore jewel-studded earrings and a matching necklace. She held what looked like a program book and a bouquet of white flowers. A black evening dress traveled the full length of her body, concealing most of her shoes. Her smile was bright and white. Caroline had laughed when she saw the cutout. "You had a crush on Di?"

"No. Maybe the queen. Elizabeth II. There's a stoicism, a beauty about her, especially in her younger pictures." Caroline laughed, and they fell onto the bed, beginning to fuck.

Diana had died in a car crash. Looked like Dale would, too.

Caroline. Caroline. She was damn good in bed. Good enough for Lena keep her around months past her expiration date. The two of them had started off great. Caroline used to be full of laughter and understanding. The opposite of clingy. She had been perfect for Lena, not an easy task with Lena's crazy busy schedule of school and work.

Lena told herself she was glad they were over. Caroline had become a nag. Insecure. A mean drunk who, lately, drank way too much. Plus, the last few times they'd had sex, the magic was gone.

But Lena's chest hurt. She had loved Caroline and maybe still did. Her heart was not a switch.

Lena re-read her mother's message on the cast. Plenty of fish in the sea.

"You should've left these as your last words," Lena mumbled. She got the letter back out. How was she going to tell Caris? Her grandparents? Should she?

Lena sat at her computer. Time to type her own letter, to Caris. She would get every word right, then handwrite it to make it personal.

Caris:
I don't know where to start. Maybe six months ago, when I found out Mom was a man in a woman's body. She walked into Azizi. Midnight, Wednesday. The bar was pretty empty.

"Just water," Mom said, but I knew that.

I took a break, and we sat outside. "I love you," Mom said.

I could not say the words back. We talked a bit, and then...

"I'm like your friend Karl," Mom said. "You treat him like he's normal. I love you for that. More than you will ever know."

I did not understand at first. The realization dawned gradually, a brain cell here, a brain cell there, and...

Aw, hell. No point in typing the whole sob story. She's transgender, she asked me not to tell anyone, and she was too chicken to tell you.

Lena bit her lip, selected all the text and deleted it. She continued typing.

Caroline was right. I am in love with you. Pretty goddamned pathetic, I know. Happened the first time we met. Your smile. You smiled, a slightly lopsided grin, one end up more than the other, and held your hand out. "Lena," you said, your voice soft and delicate and eager. "I'm so happy to meet you at last."

I scrambled to my feet and shook your hand. Here I was, trying to come to grips with this sudden young woman who was engaged to my mother. I had pictured someone my mom's age. Not this. Not you. You smiled some more. Your smile did funny things to me. My heart. My stomach. I felt instantly sorry for you, though. This young beautiful woman was in for hell. I could warn you about what my mother was like in a relationship, but you probably wouldn't believe me. And Mom would be furious. She did not realize how she was. Sweet and caring and perfect at first, then later, controlling and distant.

You smiled your smile many times that night. Lucky Mom.

Here's something silly. I don't care about Mom not playing with Nakeem Joseph and Aron Michelle. (Did she tell you about them?) Sometimes, though, I picture you with them. The three of you laugh the same way. Smile the same way, too. Weird. Maybe not. After all, there are only so many ways to smile.

Whatever happens, you can do so much better than Mom. (And certainly better than me, too.) I'm jealous of Mom. The look you get in your eyes sometimes when you stare at her, and you think no one's watching...

I hope someday someone looks at me like that. I hope I look at someone like that someday.

Lena re-read what she had typed and deleted it.

Chapter 3

In the morning, Caris packed for her and Donovan's discharge. She could not wait to escape. She was claustrophobic with the hovering, as if people thought she would slit her wrists and her stomach and smear the floor with her entrails. Plus her breasts throbbed. The pain was persistent, ever-present. Her son, this child who burst from her, was greedy. He needed to go home.

Lena showed up. *Great. As if Jennifer, George, Shirley and Mom weren't enough.*

"On your way out?" Lena asked. Her face was pinched, and lines of exhaustion were etched under her eyes — which were green today. Made sense; her shirt was green.

"Going home."

"Could I have a minute alone with you?"

Once Jennifer, George, Shirley and Phyllis were out of the room, Lena proffered a gift certificate to Chili's. "Fifty dollars. I figured you wouldn't feel like cooking for a while."

Caris took it. She touched Lena's elbow lightly, to express her gratitude. "Thank you. You look nice with your hair down."

A sheepish grin. Caris enjoyed it. Lena needed to smile and laugh more. "Hard to pull my hair back with the cast."

"I have a scrunchie. Want me to pull your hair back for you?"

"Um...nah. No need."

"You sure?"

Lena sighed. "Okay. Knock yourself out."

Caris got a scrunchie and a mini-brush from her travel bag. She pulled Lena's hair back. It was sleek and shiny, and darker this close up. Smelled like strawberry. "You okay in the shower?"

"I put plastic over my cast."

"Your hair's pretty. I could braid it sometime."

"I don't do fancy."

"I know." Caris worked quickly and replaced her brush. "Thanks for yesterday," she said. She replayed Lena's warmth on hers and wished for it again. "For coming to tell me in person. It means a lot."

Lena's brows flickered. "I'm not a total Neanderthal. Although that would be cool. I'd get a lot of money making public appearances."

"You'd be the oldest woman alive."

Lena giggled — actually giggled — a strange sound coming from her.

She did not let the levity last, though. "About yesterday, I…" Lena rubbed her cheek. "My arm. I was trying to leave my apartment building, Caroline didn't want me to and was trying to block me. We got into a tussle. She accidentally pushed me down the steps. I didn't want Grandma and Granddad to hear."

Caris searched Lena's face, but Lena would not meet her gaze. Caris wanted to ask many questions: *Why are you telling me? Why were you and Caroline fighting? Was it really an accident? Did you tell the police?* Questions tended to shut Lena down, but Caris risked one. "Are you still with her?"

"No. We're done."

"Good."

"You can say it," Lena said. "Told you so."

"I'm not going to say that. Your mother was the one who —" Caris stopped. "Is the one who…"

"Yeah." Lena inclined her head. "Right. You're Switzerland. Anyway. In other words, hope you enjoy the gift card. Call me if you need me to bring food over from Chili's." Azizi, where Lena bartended, was next door to Chili's.

"You want to come tonight for dinner?"

"I have class."

"You don't have class."

Lena's nostrils flared. "You think I'd lie to you about having class? After what happened to Mom?"

"Well —"

"Shit," Lena muttered under her breath.

Caris said nothing. She could remind Lena about the lunch and coffee dates they had made when they first met. Dates to get to know each other before Caris became Lena's stepmother. Dates that Lena canceled on. Each and every one, until Caris stopped asking.

Now was not the time to bring up old history. "Don't go back to Caroline," Caris said.

"I'm not."

"I'm here if you want to talk. Anytime."

Strained smile. "Thanks. Well, see ya."

"Wait." Caris placed her hand on Lena's forearm. Lena stiffened, but Caris kept her touch where it was. She wondered what Lena was like in her natural element, with friends. Probably gregarious, witty, talkative.

"What?" Lena asked.

"When *can* you come over for dinner? Or lunch or something?"

"I'll let you know."

Great. Same old.

"I'll call. I promise. We'll have dinner. I'll let you know."

"I used to be with a woman named Susan. She was a tiny thing, but

19

she could — she really could — she gave me a black eye. The next day, she was contrite and seemed genuinely sorry. Her behavior was so abnormal, I forgave her. The next week, I got another black eye, and I was out of there. I should've left her the first time. This is serious, Lena. Domestic violence."

"I know what it's called. That's not what happened with Caroline. It was an accident."

"Okay," Caris said quietly, but something in Lena's expression scared her. Lena and Caroline had been on and off for about a year. Who wasn't to say they would be on again tonight? Lena was exhausted from this ordeal with Dale. Weak. Vulnerable. If Caroline, nice and familiar, showed up saying the right words, bearing the right gifts, wouldn't Lena be putty in Caroline's hands? Especially if the fall truly had been an accident.

Lena's life. Don't be a mother hen.

"Call me anytime or stop by anytime," Caris said. "Breakups aren't easy."

"I'm not crying into a tub of ice cream."

Caris nodded. She had gotten as far as she would with Lena.

Lena took a few steps toward the door, then turned. "Hey. What color are my eyes today?"

"Green."

Lena seemed pleased. "Good. Green is more interesting than brown."

"Didn't your mother take you to the hospital?"

Lena's green eyes turned wary. "Yes." A pause. She added: "No one else was answering their phones."

"Where was Caroline?"

"I got up and told her I was fine. I asked her to leave, and she did."

"You got up like — "

"Haven't you been in a situation where you'd do anything to get the other person to leave you alone?"

"She left just like that? Without making certain you were okay?"

Lena's cheeks flushed. "What's the big deal?"

"Do you love Caroline?"

The question gave Lena pause. "I…I…I guess."

"Here's the thing, Lena. I'm worried if she shows up, you will take her back. It can be hard to let go. If you're being abused — " Caris stopped. She was one to be talking. She would prefer the black eyes over Dale's mind games. So crazy. The past few months had been an awful roller coaster ride.

Caris started again. "If you're being abused, you don't have to be. We can figure — "

Lena snorted. "Because you got two black eyes doesn't mean I'm being abused. I can handle myself. And so what if I take her back? What's it to you?"

"We're family. Why else did you tell me what happened with her?"
Lena narrowed her eyes. "Goodbye."

*****

The throbbing in her breasts was unceasing. Caris had never hated milk more. *Moo. Moo.*

Traffic was good for the drive from Inova Fairfax to the townhouse on Rundale Court. Caris looked at grass beginning to turn green with the promise of spring. At boring old suburbia. Strip malls. Seven-Elevens. Starbucks. Couples with dogs. With children. She could be anywhere. She could be in, say, Boston. Long Island. Oklahoma City. She was not necessarily in Northern Virginia. *Dale won't be home. How can that be? Three days ago, she was walking around, living...fucking someone else?*

Stop at Baskin-Robbins.

Stop at the mall.

Stop at the flower shop.

Go to Dulles. Buy plane tickets for somewhere. Anywhere that's not here. I bet Rome is good this time of year.

"We're here," Phyllis said.

Caris wandered upstairs to the nursery. Her breasts could wait a few more minutes. She and Dale had not finished the nursery, but the necessities were complete. Crib, fresh green paint on the walls, diaper changing table, rocking chair. Baby book. Caris slumped to the floor, pressing the book to her lips. The leathery kiss of dead cow failed to comfort her. No faux leather for Dale. First-class all the way for Daelyn Ismay, yes sir. Always.

About a year ago, Dale had arrived home, with a gift. "Here," Dale said, an impish light in her expression.

"A baby book?"

Dale beamed. "Let's have a baby soon. What do you say?"

Confusion washed through Caris. Before their wedding, before their engagement really, they had talked about kids. They had decided they would adopt an older child, especially given Dale's age. Fine with Caris. She had no overwhelming desire to get pregnant. She could take it or leave it. Lots of pros to not getting pregnant: no weight gain, no pain, intact body. Lots of older kids needed love and homes.

"A baby?" Caris asked. "Do you mean—"

"Let's look at sperm donors."

"A baby," Caris repeated. She would not bring up the issue of Dale's age. Life was unpredictable. She could die years before Dale. There was work, though. Caris was making inroads in her job, with her promotion to

—
21

manager.

Dale deflated. "I was at the park today on my lunch break. Really cute kid there, maybe a year old. He kept saying 'Mama!' 'Mama!' I realized that…" Dale's cheeks flushed. "Stupid, huh? Never mind. His smile was, I don't know. He looked like Lena. Hard to explain. When she was younger, Lena was magic in my life. Having magic again would be nice. Not that I'm saying you're not magical. You're magic, baby."

Dale rarely was at a loss for words and hated to show weakness. *This is serious. For real.* "Sure," Caris said. What difference did a few years make? Work would always be there. Family came first.

Dale grinned, her eyes lighting up in a way Caris saw only occasionally. The light was pure, unbridled, joyous. If a baby was magic, maybe the magic was already starting.

The first page of the baby book held four pictures: Dale and Caris, two months pregnant, four months pregnant, six months pregnant and from only last week, eight months pregnant. The next few pages showed photos from the baby shower and copies of a couple of sonograms. Caris flipped back to the first page, focusing on the photo of her two months pregnant, her baby bump truly only a bump. Dale beamed in a pinstripe business suit and purple tie. Her hand protectively covered Caris's stomach. The photo was taken just before their marriage nosedived.

That was another life. Yesterday was another life.

Caris wanted to cry. Tried to cry. Could not. *I'll cry when the phone call comes. It's happened. Your wife passed away. Peacefully.*

*****

Lena liked the middle school Nakeem Joseph and Aron Michelle attended, although she wondered if they felt out of place there. Nakeem and Aron lived in Silver Spring, Maryland, and their school was full of white faces. Nakeem and Aron were fairly dark, although Aron was lighter than Nakeem. Just a bit lighter.

Nakeem's baseball game was in the third inning when Lena arrived, and he was manning third base. Easy to tell which one he was: the only black face. For that reason too, identifying Aron and her parents in the stands was easy. Lena sat as far from them as possible. She wore big sunglasses and a hat. She was in no way interested in interacting with Malik and Joanna Soundros. Nor with Nakeem or Aron, for that matter, because she was not supposed to be here. She was not staying long. The longer she stayed, the more risk of one of the Soundroses seeing her. Malik had given her the schedule for Nakeem's games, probably without

Joanna's knowledge. Malik was a good guy, a great guy. Joanna was a wonderful parent too, and if Lena were in her place, Lena might be acting the same way.

Lena had lied to Caris. Course she had. What was she supposed to say: *This kid Nakeem, whom you don't know and never will, although he has a smile like yours, has a baseball game, and because of my work and school, it's probably the only game of his I'll get to see this season. So, yeah, I'm going to his game.*

Silver Spring, on a map, did not seem too far from where Lena lived in Alexandria, Virginia. Factor in D.C. traffic, though, and the trip easily could be on the far side of two hours. And that was one way.

No way Lena could have done dinner with Caris.

Lena got up to leave two innings after she arrived, after getting to see Nakeem belt out a single. He was a hustler, that one — took off like a bullet to first base and narrowly beat out the throw.

"Lena?" The call came as Lena was passing the concession stand on the way to her car. *Joanna. Shit.*

Lena pasted on a smile and turned around. Yep, Joanna, with Aron, and Aron grinned at her mother. "See, Mom, I told you that was Lena." The girl bestowed a shy smile upon Lena — the Caris smile, one end up more than the other. "Hey, Lena."

Lena stayed a few arms' lengths from the child. "Hello, Aron. Looking good."

"Like my hair? I got tired of the cornrows." The girl's hair was nappy, but not a full Afro.

"It's beautiful."

"You should've let us know you were coming," Joanna said.

"Spur of the moment decision."

"How did you know about the game?"

Lena would spare Malik. "I got a schedule from the school."

"What happened to your arm?" Aron asked.

"Clumsy me tripped down the steps. Forgot to tie a shoelace."

"Ouch."

Lena laughed. "Yes, big ouch!"

"Can I sign?"

"I don't have the right pen for it."

"Mom has one. Don't you?"

Joanna, a shadow on her features, got a Sharpie from her purse.

Aron read the messages on Lena's cast, which totaled ten by now. "You have a lot of friends."

"Don't you?"

The girl looked up at Lena and shrugged. "S'pose." Aron found a patch of white space. "I don't know what to write."

"Draw a smiley face," Joanna suggested, so that was what Aron did. She added her name too: *Aron M.* And then: *Nakeem J.*

"Perfect," Lena said. "Thank you, sweetie."

"Don't go," Aron said. "Have dinner with us after the game. Can she, Mom?"

"No, hon," Joanna said, her smile tight. "Lena has to let us know first if she's coming."

"Your mother's right," Lena said. "I'll see you soon, though, okay?"

"You won't," Aron said. "You weren't even going to say hi today."

"You and your brother are getting birthday cards a bit early," Lena said. "I mailed them today."

Aron's face lit up. "Really?"

"Thirteen years old! Come on. What a huge birthday."

"Come on, hon," Joanna said. "I'll set something up with Lena soon." She gave Lena a *look* and linked hands with her daughter. They walked off, slowly, their hips sashaying, and then Joanna laughed, and then Aron did too, and a painful, sickening heaviness constricted Lena.

Chapter 4

Throughout her pregnancy, Caris had wondered about the countless firsts coming her way. First diaper change. First breastfeed. First night at home with her baby. First time getting up in the night to answer the baby's cries. First tooth. First word. First birthday. Well, the first birthday was technically the day of the birth, right?

Caris lay in bed, facing away from Jennifer. Facing the moon, the window. Freedom. First night at home with Donovan. No crying baby. Other than gulping hungrily at her breasts, Donovan was an angel. That made Caris uneasy. She had gobbled new-mother books, devoured them. Read horror stories to prepare herself, because no matter how bad her baby might be, no matter how much he cried, fussed, spit, threw up, refused to eat, plenty of other people's babies were worse. Now she wished he would cry so she would have something to do besides think and toss and turn.

Caris gave up and trundled out of bed. Moonlight filtered through the nursery windows, cloaking Donovan in a silver spacesuit. "Hey, little alien," Caris said. She sat in the rocking chair, found a good angle through the bars of his crib, and watched him sleep. He was tiny, a fly, in his bed. Maybe she would go out tomorrow to buy a bassinet or a cradle. She probably would not go to the hospital. She would be doing everyone a favor if she stayed away from Dale. Her engagement ring and wedding ring were tucked away in the bottom drawer of her jewelry box, thanks to pregnancy bloating her fingers into Vienna sausages. Maybe these rings would wither and die in the drawer.

"I'll do the best I can," she told her son. Her chest hurt. I'm a single mother. "I'll screw up, but I'll do my best for you. By you. Always." Earlier, at the hospital, Caris had cradled Donovan and looked into his eyes. She would have liked to say love overfilled her heart, joy seized her being, all that mushy crap, but she had been too scared, too fretful, worrying about Dale.

She hauled herself from the chair and peered in at her son. His eyes fluttered open. "Hey, Donovan," she whispered.

He made a little noise, and an intense loneliness pierced Caris. She checked the time. *12:45 a.m., April 3, and I still don't feel like his mother. I don't feel like anyone.*

She went into the bathroom and slipped her shirt off. *Let's see these elephant, National Geographic breasts.* They were fascinating. She could gawk at them for hours because they were so awful. The blue veins on her breasts reminded her of the spider web on Dale's scalp. *When will I feel like a woman again?* She wet a finger with her tongue. She rubbed the slickness onto a nipple and pinched. The soreness made her cry out. Barely started breastfeeding, and she was ready to go off. She pulled her sweat pants down halfway. The stretch marks on her stomach created a forest of twigs.

Jesus Christ. Why am I torturing myself like this? No need to rub it in. She needed to assert herself, to stop letting herself and others trample her self-esteem.

Caris checked the time again. One a.m. Lena would probably be up. On the nights Lena bartended, she did not get home until past two a.m. She likely had a late bedtime every night. No more letting Lena get away with her lies. No more letting her stepdaughter look at her in the way that said: *Blond bimbo gold digger.*

Lena answered on the second ring, with a worried: "Caris?"

"I'm not an idiot," Caris snapped. "You didn't have class."

"I...but I did."

"At least have the ovaries to say to my face: 'Hey, you know what? Thanks for the dinner offer, but no thanks.' I'd rather you tell me the truth than your lies. I'm not a fucking gold digger! I loved your mother. I love your mother."

Lena did not reply for a long while, but the silence was strangely reassuring. As long as Caris was on the phone, she would not have to return to Jennifer. Or to Donovan. Or seek refuge in an empty living room.

"I know," Lena whispered. "I know, Caris. I'm glad she had you."

Caris reached for Dale's toothbrush. Its bristles were fraying. Maybe that was why Dale had not taken it to the Holiday Inn.

"Are—are you okay?" Lena asked. "I mean, uh, considering."

"Your mother needs a new toothbrush."

"Oh."

Another silence. Caris sat on the toilet. She lifted her gaze to the shower curtains, which were navy blue. Solid.

Boring.

Dale had picked them out, and Caris suddenly preferred something bright. Colorful.

"Well, I'll, you know, I'll get her a toothbrush tomorrow," Lena said. "One of these fancy electric ones, right? What color should I get?"

Tears sprang to Caris's eyes, and she wiped them away. Lena was sweet. Humoring her. Pretending Dale would need a toothbrush again one day. Well, hell. Lena was probably doing it for herself too. Maybe Caris ought to play along.

"I guess blue," Lena went on. "It's still her favorite color, right?"

"Like the shower curtains."

"Okay. The shower cur—okay."

"She hasn't used electric toothbrushes in a while."

"I'll get a regular one."

Caris heaved herself up. Time to try to sleep again. Time to face reality again. "Don't worry about the toothbrush. I'll get it. Anyway, I better go. Hope I didn't wake you."

"I don't mind getting the toothbrush. And you didn't wake me."

Something in Lena's voice gave Caris pause. Something sad. Something lonely. "What were you doing?"

Lena sighed, long and heavy. "Just looking at pictures."

"Of your mom?"

"No, uh, just..."

Ah. "Caroline."

"No. Look, Caris, I'll call soon. I promise. We'll do dinner or something."

"Okay," Caris said slowly. "Okay."

*****

Shirley arrived about nine o'clock in the morning, unannounced. "Want to go to the hospital with me?"

"Where's George?" Caris asked.

"He stayed with Dale last night."

Caris avoided the earlier question. "I'm getting a bassinet or cradle for Donovan. The crib swallows him up."

"Good idea. I'll go with you, then we'll visit Dale. Having Donovan with her will be good medicine."

"Don't know if he'll be allowed in her room."

"We'll find out."

"Shirley." Caris reached for her mother-in-law's shoulder, trying to convey gentleness in the touch. "It's best if I don't see Dale right now."

Disapproval puckered Shirley's lips. "You saw her already."

"Yes, to tell her the baby's name and to show her a picture."

Shirley fished a tube of lipstick from her purse. "Revlon. Best brand."

"Okay."

"My daughter loves you."

"Maybe. She hasn't been treating me well."

Shirley applied her lipstick and carefully replaced the tube. "Dale needs you right now. Put everything else aside."

Caris could not verbalize her answer. *Dale called me a fucking idiot for miscalculating a decimal point. She called me a whore like my mother because she thought I was flirting with a grocery store clerk. And that's just two in a long list.* Caris could not simply grin and pretend nothing happened.

"Is she cheating?" Shirley asked.

"Probably."

Shirley steered Caris to the couch. "Dale's not perfect. She makes mistakes. All people do."

Caris had a feeling what Shirley would say next. Probably George had cheated, Shirley had kicked him out, they had fought, but eventually found their way back together.

"When I was younger, I cheated on George," Shirley said quietly.

Caris tried to find Shirley's eyes, but Shirley avoided her. "I made a mistake and hurt George immensely. It took a couple of years for him to trust me again, but you know what? I cheated. I still loved him with all my heart. The cheating did not mean I loved him less. My husband and I fought for each other and learned from our mistakes. Dale's the other mother of your son. She loves you. I remember when she called to announce she was engaged. She'd never sounded happier. She went on and on about you, your hair, your laugh, your eyes, your humor."

"Why'd you cheat?"

Shirley brought out her Revlon again. "I was lonely. George was in the army and overseas."

"Oh."

Shirley patted Caris's leg. "So," Shirley said. "We'll buy the bassinet or cradle—my treat—and go to the hospital."

"All right," Caris mumbled. She would stay five minutes and leave. If Caris seeing Dale for five minutes would help her grieving mother-in-law, Caris could do that.

Dale looked much the same as she had the day before. Same spider web of a head, same everything. However, George looked like he had aged ten years. Shirley handed over a key to the hotel room where they were staying. "Room 341. See you tonight." They kissed goodbye—quick pecks on the lips—and Caris searched for love in George's eyes, in Shirley's eyes. Did not find it.

When Caris got home, a plastic Safeway bag was hanging from the front door. Dale's toothbrush. Lena had not forgotten.

*****

The next week was a haze for Lena. She worked. She went to classes. She avoided her family, most of all Caris. Lena felt like a cancerous tumor was gnawing at her stomach. *You have to tell Caris, you have to…*

Two weeks after the car wreck, Lena's cancer was unbearable. She woke up at eight a.m., before the alarm, and reached for the picture. She had a new morning habit. She would retrieve the photo from her nightstand top drawer. Wedding photo, only picture Lena had of Caris. Her lips had playful, dancing corner and a sly knowledge. Sensuality brimmed. Her strapless dress gave way to a delicious swell of breasts. Her curves were shapely and seductive.

This morning, Lena studied the photo until her alarm went off at ten minutes after eight. Caris's smile and her mysterious expression were easy to get lost in.

Lena had to tell her. Soon, before the cancer devoured Lena's stomach. *Mom was transgender. And she tried to kill herself. I mean, he tried to kill himself. Kind of. Ugh.* She was so bad with the pronouns.

Lena could not bring herself to ring the townhouse doorbell, though. She told herself it was because her grandparents had moved in with Caris for the time being. Telling Caris with Shirley and George around would not do. Caris would need time to work through the revelations at her own pace, and they could decide together if or when to tell Shirley and George. The other, more real reason Lena was scared: Caris was accessible now, she was different. The change was slight, but it was there. Definitely there.

Lena kept replaying the intensity in Caris's eyes during their conversation about domestic violence. Caris's touch on Lena's arm.

Before, Caris would not have touched her.

Caris had looked awful, no doubt about it. Purplish suitcases under her eyes. Limp hair. Until the car wreck, Caris had been too beautiful, too perfect, she had been elevated, she had been Lena's mother's wife. This post-pregnancy, grieving Caris was different. The old Caris would never have called Lena at one a.m.

Lena padded into the kitchen to get her cellphone. She found Caris's number in her cell address book and pressed it.

Caris answered on the third ring with a pleased, surprised: "Lena. Hi."

Lena's heart fluttered. *Brisk. Businesslike.* Her gaze strayed to the trash can, where she had dumped a bouquet of calla lilies two days ago. The flowers were from Caroline. They came with a card reading: *Love always, Caroline.*

"Caris, hello," Lena said. "Did you get the toothbrush?"

"Yep. Thank you."

Part of Lena ached to explain everything right then, about Nakeem and Aron and that one stupid night with Deonte, and that she had been looking at the children's pictures when Caris called at one a.m., but the cautious part of Lena won. "Are you free tomorrow night for dinner at my place?"

Chapter 5

"I'm not here to see you," Caris told Dale later that day. "Not really. I have an appointment with a shrink across the street. Figured I'd stop in."

No response.

"No, it wasn't my idea. Jennifer's. You know how she is. Therapy heals all wounds. She recommended him. Figured I'd give it a try."

Did she imagine that Dale's right eyelid twitched?

"Dr. Mark Lukaas. He's a big-name gay psychologist. Supposedly. I'd never heard of him."

The eyelid twitched again, and Caris squeezed Dale's hand.

Coma. Odd word. A heavy, multi-layered blend of four letters that struck fear in so many hearts. Yet it reminded Caris of a condiment. *I'd like ketchup, pickles and a touch of coma with my hamburger, please. Wait. Sir! An extra packet of coma, please. Mmm! How about that coma. What's the secret sauce?*

Not only was Dale in a coma, she was likely paralyzed from the waist down. *May I have combo #3 please? A chicken sandwich with paralysis – partial, please – and a side of coma fries.*

Shirley said it was a miracle that the injuries from the crash had not killed Dale. There was no "yet" with Shirley. Dale was going to live and be okay, and that was all there was to it. "It's a sign from God," she argued. "God's telling us Dale is a miracle. There will be more miracles." Whenever Shirley went on like that, George looked away, a shadow in his eyes.

Caris was not buying the spiel either. She wondered what exactly her mother-in-law saw. Was she in denial, thinking that as long as she prayed and praised God, Dale would be okay? Shirley's religion was as newfound as a baby's smooth bottom. Before the accident, Caris had never heard Shirley use the word "God" except in occasional phrases such as "God damn it!" *Foxhole atheist.* As for Caris's religious inclinations, she was not sure and was in no hurry to find out. She was drained, exhausted. She was a girl Pinocchio going through the motions, yearning to be human – yearning to connect with her son and yearning to understand the person she had married.

"Bye," Caris said, and Dale's eyelid twitched goodbye.

*****

Fifteen minutes later, Dr. Mark Lukaas said: "Not only are you a brand new mother, your wife is in the hospital, unresponsive. And she had been emotionally abusive. And probably cheating." A deep frown etched his face. Maybe because Caris had been thirty minutes late. "So, you're dealing with a lot of emotions."

Einstein. "Right."

"Were you satisfied with her before the emotional abuse began?"

"Uh…" Caris's knee-jerk impulse was to say yes. And it seemed like the correct answer. "Yes. Dale used to do many things right. She massaged my feet. Cooked dinner. Made me feel loved. Looked at me with deep brown eyes and made the world safe."

"What drew you to Dale?"

"Her sharp mind. She could analyze the hell out of something, anything."

Dr. Lukkas quirked an eyebrow as if to say: *That's all?*

Caris sighed. "She projected stability. She was a rock."

"Why was that an issue?"

"When I was a child, my mother and I were always scrimping and scrounging. She was an alcoholic. Money went toward her drinks. I don't know who my father is. She blacked out and woke up pregnant." Caris clenched her right hand, hating how she was making herself sound. "The whole package drew to me to Dale, okay? My stepdaughter thought I was a gold digger. Oh, she never said so out loud, but it was pretty clear. I wasn't a gold digger, though. I loved Dale."

"Go on."

"Dale used to be a good listener. I miss telling her the little things. Like, you know, the other day I saw a poodle wearing a pink shirt and with pink bows in its hair. Really? Come on. Why do people feel the need to give poodles these ridiculous frou-frou haircuts? And names like Rocky or Keifer."

Dr. Lukaas did not laugh. Damn. *That was probably his poodle.*

"How was your sex life?" Dr. Lukaas asked.

"Okay."

"You were satisfied."

Caris hesitated before answering. "We didn't have sex after my fourth or fifth month of pregnancy. If that. Our last time, she couldn't reach orgasm. She threw a fit, blaming me. She said I needed to work on my bedroom skills and that I was a lousy lover."

"What did you say?"

Caris ignored the lump at the bottom of her throat. "I don't remember." *I don't know if I like being a mother. I don't know if I like my son.*

The timer on Dr. Lukkas' desk went off, playing a Beethoven sonata.

His frown was back, as if to say: *Please be on time next week.*

*****

The next morning, Caris and Jennifer packed up Donovan and headed to the mall.

"You excited to buy real clothes again?" Jennifer asked.

"No. Ask me again in two months, when I have more of my body back."

They went into a new store called Space. Caris had not told Jennifer that a specific event—pizza at Lena's apartment that night—was driving the shopping trip. She was not sure why. Having dinner with her stepdaughter was innocent. Maybe the hesitation was because Jennifer did not like Lena. Or maybe the hesitation was because it felt nice to have a little place to herself, a little knowledge to herself. The urge to escape, to not be Caris Ismay, to not be Dale's wife, to not be Donovan's mother, had pounded at Caris since the car accident.

When did time alone become such a bad thing? Her mother and Jennifer hovered. George had the tendency to pop up behind furniture and point out that so and so thing needed polishing or fixing up and that he would be glad to do it. Shirley was driving Caris nuts, with being always on about Dale this, Dale that: *Dale smiled today, I swear it. This is nothing, she'll be back with us soon.*

In any case, nothing wrong with wanting to buy a stain-free shirt to commemorate having dinner with someone new.

Caris plucked a dress in size eight, her pre-pregnancy size. The dress was a sleek black number that should have come to right above her knees.

"That won't fit," Jennifer said.

"Give me some credit. Looking isn't a crime." Caris grabbed a few shirts. "Be right back." She locked herself in a dressing room stall. A pumpkin was her reflection in the mirror. *Awesome. I'm a walking advertisement for Halloween.* Black sweat pants, orange T-shirt. The pinnacle of fashion. Lena's invitation for dinner had come at the perfect time.

*****

Lena had to look twice to make sure the woman who met her outside the apartment building was Caris. She looked fifty. Beaten down. Worn out. Her eyes were raccoon-like. Not so different from Lena's own eyes.

But then Caris smiled, and the twenty extra years flew off.

Lena shook off the *pitter-patter* of her heart and indicated her building. She lived only five minutes from the townhouse, but Caris had never been inside Lena's building. Perhaps she had driven by once or twice. Lena had no idea. "Welcome to my old maid among nubile virgins," she said. The house stood out among the renovated homes on the street. "I couldn't resist the color."

"Cafeteria mystery meat color is nice."

"Nice peeling, huh? Reminds me of a bad sunburn. Come on in."

Lena led Caris through the house. Lena had separate keys for the main entrance and for her own unit. No buzzers, which was why she'd had to meet Caris outside. "I'm on the second floor."

They walked up the staircase.

"These are the steps you fell down?" Caris asked.

"Yep."

"Lots of them."

"Guess so."

Once they were in the apartment, Caris looked around the living room, and Lena tried to see the apartment through Caris's eyes. Was Caris comparing the apartment and the townhouse? She probably thought Lena's place was shit compared with her own expansive townhouse. Of course, that townhouse was Dale-bought, Dale-furnished. Lena would take her apartment over the townhouse any day.

Lena was a naturally tidy person — reasonably tidy — but she had not dusted or vacuumed in a while before today. So, she had spent about an hour cleaning, and she hoped her effort was not too obvious. The scent of Pledge lingered faintly.

"You get the grand tour by standing right there," Lena said, making her voice light. "Well, except for the bathroom." From where Caris and Lena were in the middle of the living room, they could see into the bedroom. A short hallway led from the bedroom to the bathroom. The kitchen adjoined the living room. All there was to it.

The furniture was eclectic and scrounged from Goodwill. Lena did not have a true couch, but instead a loveseat. And a purple plaid Laz-Boy, a reupholstered monstrosity from the 1980s.

"I love it," Caris said.

"You do?"

Lopsided grin. "It's you, Lena."

Lena averted her gaze. Otherwise, she would look at Caris a heartbeat too long — several heartbeats too long. "We should go back outside and wait for the pizza."

"Can I use your bathroom?"

"Sure. I'll wait for the pizza."

"Lena." Caris reached for her arm. Kept her touch there.

Don't touch me. Please. "What?" Lena hoped her voice was not high or strangled.

Caris grinned. "I needed to get out of the house badly. You have no idea. Thanks for having me over."

*****

Caris unbuttoned her elephant maternity jeans and sat on the toilet. Her urination took a few seconds to get going. Hopefully there would not be blood. That had pretty much stopped, but yesterday had brought some spotting.

Lena had a couple of framed black and white pictures on the walls, of women naked, kissing and making love. Women with perfect curves, perfect bodies. Clearly exposed breasts, nipples, trimmed pussies.

Women who were not cows, who didn't moo, who did not have babies scrambling for their udders.

Black and white. That was what Caris would do when Lena told her whatever it was she needed to say. The shadow in Lena's eyes just now had told Caris that this dinner was not social. Lena had something to say about her mother. Something bad. Caris would compartmentalize and keep functioning. She would get through it.

*****

Lena was on the loveseat. "Got the pizza." She indicated the box on the coffee table.

The thought of eating, of cheese and grease and a secret, made Caris sick. But she forced a grin. "Smells great."

"Drink?"

"Do you have Sprite?"

"Coming right up."

Caris sat. What was Lena going to tell her? Dale was cheating? Dale was leaving her? *Huge surprise. Huge secret.*

Lena returned with two cans of Sprite, one tucked under her chin because of her cast. Caris grinned and lowered her gaze to the cast. Signatures smothered it. "Guess there's no room for my John Hancock."

"You can sign on top of whatever."

Caris opened both of their Sprites. "You and I, sometimes it's like

—
34

walking through a minefield. We're basically the same age. It's weird. I know."

"It is, yes."

Caris sipped from her Sprite. "I broke my leg when I was twelve. Most of my classes in middle school were on the third floor. Pain in the ass. I had to crutch up and down several times a day."

"Hmm."

"Will you come by sometime? Meet the baby."

"I met him already."

Caris felt a muscle twitch at her jaw. *You met him for one second.*

"Shit," Lena muttered. "That came out wrong. I meant — yes, of course. I'll come by. Is he a good baby?"

"He was good the first few days. Now he's a crying beast."

"Lovely."

Caris leaned in, feeling the overwhelming urge to confide in someone. Lena would be a good person to tell. She didn't want kids. She wouldn't get that *look* in her eyes. That look of surprise, disappointment. Well, hopefully. "I don't feel like his mother. Like a mother," Caris said.

A searching gaze. Shifting browns and greens. Lena smelled good. Citrus spray, maybe.

"I feel like I'm on *Candid Camera.* I'm acting. I hold him, and I can tell he's cute. He's sweet. I pat him, I rock him, I breast feed him. But there's a part of my heart that tells me I'm missing something."

"Do you have postpartum depression?"

"I don't think so. I looked up the symptoms. Agitation or irritability. Changes in appetite. Feelings of worthlessness or guilt. Thoughts of death or suicide. A long list of blah blah blah. Trouble sleeping. *That* one I have. My doctor says to just give it time."

"You're dealing with a lot. My mom and all."

"Can you sleep? What's your trick?"

"No trick." Lena indicated the bruises under her eyes. "Seriously, do you think this is makeup? You think I go around looking like this for the fun of it?"

Caris laughed. "I'm up all night. Either pacing and thinking, waiting for the baby to cry, and then trying to calm him down, or wondering how your grandmother can snore so loud. Your mother somehow made snoring elegant. Not your grandmother. She's a bulldozer. An artillery tank. A machine gun."

"It doesn't bother Granddad?"

"He sleeps on the couch. The pull-out."

"Oh."

"Yeah. So at night, I can't even go down and lay out on the couch or watch TV. I'm stuck in my bedroom. Ahh. I don't mean to talk negative.

Shirley is at the hospital a lot of nights, and George sleeps in the spare bedroom then. So I do have plenty of opportunity for crappy late-night TV. Your grandparents are a great help. Wonderful with the baby."

Lena offered a tentative smile. "Good. That's good."

"Look, Lena." Caris closed her hand over Lena's non-cast hand and braced herself. "Why am I here?"

"Mom was transgender," Lena mumbled.

Caris was sure she misheard. "Pardon?"

"Mom was transgender. She told me six months ago that she was a man in a woman's body."

Caris stared at Lena a long moment, then at Lena's green curtains. They were lacy, flowing, and Caris became vaguely aware of Lena's hand still in hers. Of Lena entwining their fingers. Lena rested her back against the couch cushion and let out a little sigh.

Lena's fingers were long and slim. Their hands fit. Dale had thick, blocky fingers. Their hands had fit too, before Dale became — *Stop. Don't compare Dale and Lena like categories on an Excel spreadsheet.*

Transgender.

Really? *No way.*

Lena's hand in hers was no longer calm and reassuring. The touch burned, and scorched, like how ants under a magnifying glass on a sunny day must feel, but Caris was too shocked to do anything. For some reason, her mind traveled to the time Lena came out. Interesting: Caris had been out and proud since she was seventeen. Lena had come out to her mother and Caris only two years ago, when Lena was twenty-seven. Lena had done it in the living room at the townhouse, and Dale's mouth had fallen open.

"Gay?" Dale said in disbelief. "Oh, Lena." In a pained, displeased way. Some kind of internalized homophobia, maybe, and provoking tears from Lena. Caris tried to hug her, but Lena pushed her away. Lena had worn her green skirt then, the skirt she wore like jeans. Her shirt had been in a blue camouflage pattern. Odd combination perhaps, but on Lena, it worked.

Transgender. Transgender. The word bounced off the curtains and Caris's nonabsorbent brain. "Transgender," Caris echoed stupidly. Like Lena had said Dale was an orangutan, or a time traveler, or the secret queen of England.

"Transgender."

"Transgender." The word was a lumpy, alien object on Caris's tongue. She wanted to peel it off and hide it in one of the curtain folds. *Orangutan.* That word was better.

"Transgender," Lena said. Continuing their word tennis.

Transgender, transgender, transgender. "Really?"

Lena smiled tremulously. "Yes. Really."

Caris wondered what she should be feeling. Outrage? Betrayal? Because right now all she could think about were orangutans. Their reddish hair, shiny eyes. Their scampering. "I like your curtains. Where did you get them?"

Lena twisted her head to study her curtains. She kept her hand in Caris's, and her touch returned to being reassuring. *Don't let go, Lena. Please.*

"Target," Lena decided. "On sale."

"They're really nice. I love the color."

"Caris."

"And the word orangutan."

"What?"

"Orangutan. Like a monkey. I don't think they're monkeys, though."

"They're not."

Dale a man? Transgender? Caris reran Dale's scowls, the heated, pointed: "I am a woman. Not a man," whenever some hapless, helpful store clerk addressed her as "sir." A five-minute rant invariably followed. Reverse projecting her fears? Dale's insistence on penetrating Caris with the dildos. Refusing to let Caris penetrate her.

"Do orangutans eat pizza?" Caris asked.

"No idea."

"Can you spell orangutan?"

"O-r-a-n-g-u-t-a-n."

Pain. Exquisite pain in her breasts.

"Six months? You've known six months?"

Lena gave a helpless, despairing sigh. "If I could do it again, I'd tell you right after she told me. I wrote you a letter. Want to read it now?"

Caris should have pumped milk about five minutes ago, in the bathroom. She'd thought she could wait. But no. She'd been relatively lucky so far. Hadn't experienced severe engorgement. Elephant, weighty breasts, sore nipples, yeah, but not the swollen, rock-hard breasts many women experienced.

Oh, God. The pain caused her to bend over for a couple of seconds. She felt like she might pass out. "I have to pump. My breasts are killing me. I won't be long." Caris got to her feet and grabbed her baby bag. She closed the bathroom door behind her but did not lock it. She took her shirt off. Under it, she wore a low-cut top. She sat on the toilet. She clamped her jaw shut and mashed her teeth together. Shit. The pain infiltrated every part of her.

She pulled the left side of her shirt down first. The cup of her bra was detachable, and she attached the pump. It was manual, and Caris squeezed. She would be maybe five minutes. Because she wanted to stop breastfeeding, she just needed to relieve the pressure. Draining her breasts dry would simply signal them to produce more milk.

A tentative knock at the door. "You okay?"

"Fine. Moo."

"Did you say 'Moo?' "

"Yes. Moo. Get it? I'm expressing milk."

"Anything I can do?"

"I'm fine. I'm a cow, okay? But relatively fine."

"I don't think you're fine."

"You think I'm slitting my wrists or something? That I keep a butcher knife in my baby bag? I'm a milk cow, not a meat cow. I'm fine, Lena. This is normal."

"Can I come in?"

"No."

"Why?"

"Because. My nipples will scar you. They were nice and sweet before the baby. Now they're..." Caris looked down. Backforthbackforth motion. "They're gigantic darting minnows."

"I won't look," Lena said. "Or you could cover yourself with a towel."

Fine, fine. Caris switched breasts and draped her first shirt over her chest. "Come in if you must."

Lena edged in, clasping a tote bag. "Your virgin eyes are protected," Caris said.

Lena smiled uncertainly and perched herself on the edge of the tub. "I didn't want you to be alone."

"Yes, well."

"Do, uh..." Lena watched the slowly rising level of milk in the collection bottle with a mixture of fascination and dismay. "Interesting contraption." Meaning a scary-as-shit contraption.

"Like I said. Moo."

"Moo. Yeah."

Lena leaned in, and her knee brushed Caris's. "I guess you're okay. Should I leave you alone?"

"Do you want to be alone?"

"I—no. Do you?"

"No."

Lena kept her touch where it was, and Caris was glad for the contact. Glad for the distraction. Caris suddenly ached, not only her breasts, but all of her, for someone to lay with in bed and laugh with and cuddle with. Kiss, too. Laugh and kiss. Not sex. She was nowhere near ready for sex.

"I like your pictures," Caris said.

Lena smiled.

"Sometimes I imagine myself in a field, grazing the grass," Caris said.

"I used to be like the women in these pictures."

Another smile. Slight. "For what it's worth, cows are cute. They have their own charm. You know what? I'll put a cow picture up tomorrow."

Something in Lena's grin drew Caris in. "What's their charm?"

"I love their eyes. Have you ever looked into a cow's eyes?"

"Somehow I neglected to do that."

"When I was in middle school, we took a trip to a farm. The cows there were for making cheese. They were a brown-orange kind — the cows, not the cheese. I petted the cows. They made me feel calm. Peaceful. Their eyes were soothing, like they were saying everything would be all right. And their ears were so cute. Stuck out. Anyway." Lena chuckled self-consciously, and redness colored her cheeks. "I'll put up a cow picture tomorrow."

She's lovely. "You're saying my ears stick out," Caris teased.

Lena's blush deepened.

Caris retuned to the pictures. One pair of women was French kissing. *When will I kiss again like that?* "I went to a shrink yesterday. Dr. Mark Lukaas. He's gay. You know him?"

"No. Not crazy about shrinks."

"Me either. And definitely not him. He's Dr. Frowny Face. It's like someone forgot to take a dildo out of his ass."

Lena laughed. "Oh, boy."

"Your mom worried about you."

Lena rolled her eyes.

"She loved you. She really did. She had a hard time showing it. She wanted you to settle down, be happy and — "

"Did she tell you about Nakeem and Aron?"

"Who?"

Lena rotated her cast and pointed to two names: Aron M. Nakeem J. "Did my mother tell you about them?"

"No. Who are they?"

"Never mind. Doesn't matter. Look, Mom left me a note. The wreck was on purpose. Here. Let me show you."

Chapter 6

Lena watched and waited as Caris read. Caris's eyes moved quickly, scanning the lines. Then she stopped, her gaze turning incredulous. Unseeing. She'd stopped squeezing long ago. At last, she detached the collection bottle. She handed the note back to Lena, but in a way that signaled she was not quite registering Lena's presence.

Caris removed the shirt — deep purple — that had been covering her breasts, and the shirt fell into her lap. Lena could not help but *look*. Caris's bra had no cups, and her nipples were big. No way around it. And erect, very erect. Lena's breasts had been worse. She never breastfed Nakeem or Aron, they had gone to Malik and Joanna right away, but stopping production of breast milk had taken a few weeks.

Lena forced her eyes up.

"Still think cows are cute?" Caris asked.

"Nothing wrong with them." And there wasn't. The nipples possessed their own strange beauty, and Caris's breasts were full, round. Lovely. Lena felt stirrings of arousal between her legs. *Oh, hell.*

Caris sighed. "Damn. Look at that. My left breast is bigger. When I thought they couldn't get any worse."

Lena refused herself a second gaping. "They looked the same size to me. Your bra is cool."

Caris laughed, but in a weary way. "Gonna be a long time before a woman finds them fit to be touched again."

"You have nothing to worry about," Lena said. "You're beautiful. You really are. If that's the worst of it, then — please. You're fine. Totally fine."

Caris only laughed again. More wearily.

Lena wanted to make her feel better. She knew exactly how Caris was feeling. "I'd touch them."

"Why?"

"Um...because. Breasts are breasts. Beauty comes in many, uh, they weren't that bad, uh, they, of course I didn't see what they were like before you got pregnant, so — " *Stop. You're making it worse.*

Caris offered a smile. "Well, thank you, Lena." She put her bra cups back on and pulled her shirt up.

Lena had never told anyone about Nakeem and Aron. She was not even sure her grandparents knew. Maybe her mother had told them, maybe not, but the secret of the children, of Aron's smiley face and their names on her cast, was sour. Always had been. "Look, Caris, your breasts will get better. Mine did."

There. She had said it. Something close enough, anyway. And she felt better right away. She had nothing to be ashamed of. Teenagers made stupid mistakes. Nothing to be ashamed of at all.

"Yours got better? What do you mean?"

Lena indicated the names with her finger. *Aron M. Nakeem J.* "Like I said. My breasts got better."

Caris's eyes were wide. Wider than at the hospital, when Lena told her about the accident, and wider than just now with the transgender news. "You had a baby?"

"Two. Twins. Boy and girl. You're right that I didn't have class two weeks ago. I'm sorry I lied to you. I didn't mean to hurt you. I went to his baseball game. He hit a single. He should've been out at first, but he ran like hell."

Caris studied the names on the cast for a long, long time. Long enough for Lena's tongue to thicken and her heart to harden.

Long enough for her to realize what an idiot she was.

Lena reached into her tote bag and jammed a letter into Caris's hands. "This explains the transgender stuff. Thanks for coming over."

"Lena—"

"Go, Caris. Please."

"You have children, you have—oh, wow. How old? I thought you didn't want kids."

"I don't have children."

"Of course you had to go to the game. Yes, of course. He's your son." *Your son. Your son.*

"I told you," Lena said. "I don't have children. I'm not their mother."

"Then who are you?"

"I don't know. I'm Lena. Lena who sees them a few times a year. Officially, anyway. Unofficially I go to games and events sometimes and hide and—" *Shit, shit.* Why was she running her mouth like this? Caris was not the person to talk to. Lena got up. She went into the kitchen and began emptying the dishwasher.

Caris came in a moment later. "Lena," Caris said, and her voice was soft and delicate like the first time they had met, and Lena had no choice but to look up into Caris's eyes. She saw yearning there, or at least she thought she did. It was quite possible she was simply projecting her own desires. "You should go, Caris."

"Can I hug you goodbye?"

A hug? Her breasts pressing into Caris's, their heartbeats mingling, their—nope. Lena shook her head.

"Do you have pictures of them? How old are they? Does your mom know about them?"

"Of course she does. I don't know if Grandma and Granddad do." Up went a plate into the cabinet. A pot went in the drawer under the oven.

"Lena—"

"Later. I'll tell you more later. You should go home and read the letter explaining the transgender stuff."

Caris retrieved a fistful of spoons and forks, and Lena indicated which drawer they should go into. They worked until the dishwasher was empty, and then Caris said: "Who is their father?"

Lena sighed, fatigue snaking into her pores. "Joanna is their mother. Malik is their father. Deonte is...he's the only guy I've had sex with."

"Where did you meet him?"

"At a party. We were both fifteen years old and stupid and bored and drunk."

Caris reached for Lena.

Aw, hell. "Let me go."

"Lena, let me help you. Please? I want to hear about the kids."

"No."

Caris slid an arm, then another, around Lena's waist. She rested one hand in the small of Lena's back. Caris's breath was hot. Wonderfully alive. Their breasts pressed into each other. No use for Lena to protest further. They stayed entwined for a few minutes, and Lena was in agony. Torture. Caris with her felt good. Right.

Caris drew back a bit, her arms still around Lena, and smiled her lopsided smile. "I don't know about you, but I feel better."

Lena moved without thinking. She brushed her mouth against Caris's, only then becoming conscious of what she was doing, her every nerve meltingly aware of where Caris's warm body touched hers. Half of her said to pull back, but the other half pressed on.

Caris responded with a shiver and a soft moan. Lena let her lips graze Caris's for a long second, and then she flicked her tongue against Caris's mouth, tracing its soft fullness.

They were together, their bodies, very together, so tight they meshed as one. They kissed deeply, leisurely, in sync, no sloppiness, though there was plenty of tongue. Tangling, exploratory, playful. It was a passion Lena had not experienced before. A serious, solemn passion that reached down through her, through her heart, stomach, lungs, to her toes. A passion that acknowledged that they were kissing to get their minds off other matters, Dale for Caris, and for Lena, Nakeem and Aron, but they were kissing, they were feeling, they were alive. They kissed with a passion that acknowledged they could never be together and that this might well be their first *and* last kiss. Intimate. Sweet. Tender. Lena had never imagined Caris would be like this. This good. This perfect. Many things clicked inside Lena, not at the same time, but a little after another, the click click

click of dominoes.

This was what it was supposed to be like.

This. This. She and Caris kissed, Lena was not sure for how long, maybe five minutes, maybe ten, maybe fifteen. Then it was over. Caris drew aside, close enough for her breath to be hot on Lena's cheek, but far enough for finality. "Oh, Lena," Caris said. She sounded like she might cry. "I don't know what came over—I better go."

Lena felt like crying herself. *We made a mistake. A huge mistake.* The kiss had been the best of Lena's life. They could not just let it go. But of course they would.

*****

Caris spent the next few days on her laptop. She did not use the TV because George and Shirley would see. She watched DVDs of her and Dale: their wedding, vacations, and so on. Searching for clues that Dale was transgender. Finding nothing.

Sometimes anger burned inside her, like a low fire. Other times, she was exhausted and numb. On their wedding video, they cut the cake and smeared each other's faces. Dale had nothing but long kisses and romantic words for her. At three minutes and ten seconds into the video, Dale playfully grabbed Caris's ass. Caris, wedding dress and all, chased Dale around the reception hall and tackled her.

The present-day Caris felt like smashing a vase. How could Dale think that mistreating her for six months was preferable to telling her that Dale was transgender? Was it preferable for Dale to kill herself?

When Caris got sick of watching videos, she Google imaged "cows." Lena was right. Cows had deep, soulful eyes. Caris found a picture of two brown-orange cows, maybe the kind Lena had petted at the cheese farm or whatever kind of farm it was. Looking into their eyes helped Caris re-orient herself. Helped subside her anger toward Dale.

Caris tried her best not to think about Lena. About that kiss. That connection, that *whatever*, was what she and Dale had been missing, but Caris refused to let herself dwell on the realization. She had been caught up in emotion. She did not have that type of connection with Lena. No way, no how.

However, the fact was that Caris still felt her fingers entwined with Lena's. Still felt Lena's warmth, Lena's awed eyes on her breasts, Lena's pained voice when she talked about the children. A curious swooping pull had begun between Caris's legs during their kiss and had not gone away yet. It lingered, barely there sometimes, more there other times. Caris was tempted to laugh. Barely two weeks after having a baby, she should not be feeling any stirrings of desire.

But sure enough, that's what this was. For *Lena*. Caris rationalized away her reaction. No big deal. After months of coolness at Dale's hands, Caris was desperate for warmth. All this was. A physical reaction toward a woman who was doing her a favor by pretending to find her attractive. By pretending that cows were cute.

Lena was not attracted to her. Nope. Lena had avoided her four years because Caris was her age and a possible gold digger — not because she was attracted to Caris, to her mother's wife. Right?

Best to think about Dale. Dale was a more-immediate problem. Never mind that every time Caris closed her eyes, she replayed Lena's arms around her, Lena's cast pressing into her side. Her own arms around Lena. Their kiss. The sensation was so intense Caris felt like she and Lena parted a mere five minutes ago.

Caris had always prided herself on being open-minded. What if Dale had told her about the transgender thing? Caris played out such a conversation in her mind.

Caris, I feel like a man in a woman's body. I'm not happy. I'm transgender.
stunned silence

Here is a book you might like to read. Some information I printed off the Internet. Here's a support group. I love you, Caris, no matter what, and you're the most important person in my life.

Caris stopped at that point. The truth was, she had no idea how she would have reacted, but she did know that back then, she had loved Dale and would have done anything in her power to make sure Dale was happy and to love Dale to the best of her ability. Dale should have told her. She really should have. She should have given Caris a chance. That was what marriage was about. Trust. Faith. Poor Dale. Caris tried to imagine Dale's suffering, but her own anger got in the way.

She cancelled her next appointment with Dr. Lukaas. She needed time to digest the information before she could tell anyone. She kept slipping DVDs into her laptop and kept looking at pictures of cows. Her brain told her to let it go, she and Dale were done, but she still demanded answers. Concrete answers, not disturbing emotions.

She read Lena's letter many times. Perhaps read was the wrong word. Studied it, maybe. Admired it — the purple ink, the way Lena combined both print and cursive, the way Lena couched some phrases.

Caris:
I don't know where to start. Maybe six months ago, when I found out Mom was a man in a woman's body. She walked into Azizi. Midnight, Wednesday. The bar was pretty empty.

"Just water," Mom said, but I knew that.

I took a break, and we sat on a bench in front of Chili's. Wasn't too cold. We had our jackets.

"You're not answering your calls," Mom said.

"I've been busy. School's nuts."

"Caris is pregnant," Mom said. "About two and a half months."

I said something like: "Oh. Congratulations. I guess." I had not known you were trying to have a baby.

Mom's chin trembled and her eyelashes wavered. "Yes. Thanks."

"You don't look happy about it."

"I never meant for it to happen."

"Huh?"

"Lena." The misery in Mom's word was so acute that it caused a pain in my heart.

"What?"

"I love you."

I could not say the words back.

"She's the one. Caris is the one. The love of my life."

"Congrats."

Mom ran a hand through her hair. Tugged at her tie. "I have to tell her something. I'm afraid I'm going to lose her."

I stood. "I have to go back. See you later."

I was not doing that to be rude. You have no idea how it was for me living with Mom when I was in middle school and high school. She had several live-in relationships. They all started great. Went sour eventually. Mom would break up with them, and more than once I was the one who had to comfort these women.

This situation with you was giving me that same awful feeling, hence me wanting to get away.

Mom grabbed my arm. "You know your friend Karl?"

"What about him?"

"I'm like him."

I did not understand at first. The realization dawned gradually, a brain cell here, a brain cell there. I sat back down, my chest heavy, but my brain cells coordinating frantically. Searching memory banks for clues. Finding a few. I thought about touching Mom, some gesture of comfort on her shoulder, but we don't have that kind of relationship.

Tears sprung to Mom's eyes. I shifted away from her. Had never seen Mom cry, did not want to start now. "I was going to tell Caris. I went to the mall to buy her a gift. Sweeten her up. I saw a baby book instead and thought: 'Let's have our baby.' And then Caris became pregnant on the second try, and...we're done. Our marriage is over. I can't tell her."

"Why are you telling me?"

"I don't know," Mom said. "But I see how you are with Karl. He's—he's normal to you."

"He is. He's normal. So are you. All right?"

The next day, Mom and I met Karl for lunch. Mom was in tears most of the lunch, hot, wet, wild tears in this upscale Italian place, people staring at us, and all I could do was plan my escape route, stare and fidget and thank God that Karl was able to hug her.

This strange person who looked like Mom was doing...this. Being human. Crying. Instead of acting like a god.

Mom told her story and listened to Karl's story, which was similar to hers. Several suicide attempts, two for Karl, and for Mom, three, all shortly after my father died. I so did not need that information about Mom. She can't be distant all my life then all of a sudden, let me in with a flood of information and expect me to be instantly warm and understanding and a doting daughter.

Anyway, Karl's story had a happy ending. "Yours can too," he said.

"I'd lose my job. Mom and Dad would be devastated. And Caris..."

"She deserves to know," I put in. Basically my first comment of the lunch. "She's your wife."

"I know she's my wife!" Mom said, and her nose had a dripdripdrip.

Karl spoke up: "I'll go with you to your first therapy appointment. We'll figure out a way to tell Caris." People considering sex changes are required to undergo at least ninety days of therapy before they start hormones. They have to be fully resolved to their new identities and tell their families.

Karl and Mom met a few times on their own. Fine with me. Let him deal with her. Sometimes Mom came into Azizi while I was on duty, sometimes to talk to just me, sometimes to Karl.

I made a conscious effort, first in my thoughts and later in my conversations with Karl, and with Mom, to refer to Mom in the masculine. But I couldn't call him "Dad." Reginald Ismay is my father. Daelyn Ismay is my mother. Mom didn't want me to call her "Dad," and I was glad. I'm going to try again with the masculine now that hopefully you've had time to absorb this information.

I apologize if the rest of this letter is a confusing mix of him/his/she/her. I slip a lot.

I guess I'm really apologizing to Mom. Mom, I'm sorry I slipped sometimes. I meant no disrespect. It's taken me a while to deal and get used to this.

I would like to say that Mom's secret brought us closer, and apparently he thought it did. We spent more time together. Inside, though, I was just... I don't know. Scared. More compartmentalized about my feelings for Mom.

So, Almond's. To Mom's credit, he didn't lecture me about Caroline. We were pretty quiet, but he told me about the fight with you. You wanted to know why he was freezing you out. You thought perhaps he was cheating. You wanted a separation if things were not going to change.

Mom told me some things he had done to you. Criticizing your everything, even the way you walked, your shoes making a squeek squeek.

"I'm leaving her," Mom said.

I stayed quiet. Mom had rejected his girlfriends before they could hurt her. Was going to do the same to you and did not have the guts to explain why. I went to the bathroom and hoped Mom would be gone when I got back. No such luck.

At last, I said: "You're a coward. You want to be a man, grow some balls."

"I know," he said. He gulped down a glass of water. Got up to leave. "You coming to the hospital?"

"No." I wanted nothing to do with Mom anymore.

"Please understand, Lena. I can't lie to that baby. I can't look into that baby's eyes and be a fraud for yet another person. I can't lie anymore. Caris is going to need you after I—" he cleared his throat. "After I leave her. I'd really appreciate it if you..."

"You want me to tell her for you. I'm not. Guess what, though? She'd understand. She'd try to, anyway. She loves you. I see it in her eyes every damn time you're together! If she's the one, what the fuck are you doing leaving her?"

Mom smiled, just a little. "She wouldn't understand."

"You won't know until you tell her."

Mom studied me, her gaze dark and intense. She hugged me a long, long moment. Cried a little.

Guess she knew it could be our last hug. Her last-ever hug.

"I love you, Lena," she said, and yet again, I could not say it back.

You know, now that I think about it, I don't remember ever telling Mom I love her.

Mom thinks I have commitment problems. You probably think I do, too. Could be. I fall in love easily. Too easily. With multiple women. Lots of women at the same time. I'm young. I'll be all right. Just gotta sow oats.

Is that commitment problems? Maybe, maybe not.

I don't think I was in love with Caroline. I loved her, but that's different from being in love. Maybe that's why I was able to stay with her a year.

Anyway, I wonder what was going through Mom's mind when she pulled into the street. Maybe something like this:

He had made it fifty-six years as a woman. He could make it another fifty-six as a woman.

Or: He was an unmoored mess. The plan to continue being a woman would never succeed. He looked left one last time and on impulse, pulled out. The actions he had to take were clear. The Cadillac was sturdy. Great air bag. Firm seat belt. The truck wasn't moving fast. He would survive. Be very banged up, probably. But he would survive. I would find the "suicide" note in my tote bag and tell you all that he was a man. You would stay with him. You and Grandma and Granddad and the law firm would be so relieved he was alive, you would forgive anything.

I really don't think she meant to die. The wreck was a cry for attention. Maybe I should have just told you. The wreck could have been avoided. All this could have been avoided.

Whatever happens, you can do so much better than Mom. I should have encouraged Mom to leave you from the start, when you were two months pregnant, because you do deserve better. I'm jealous of Mom. The look you get in your eyes sometimes when you stare at her, and you think no one's watching...

I hope someday someone looks at me like that. I hope I look at someone like that someday.

-Lena

Chapter 7

Lena lay in bed, unable to sleep. As usual. As always — since the car wreck. She had just gotten off the phone with Malik and Joanna. Dinner next week at an Applebee's in Silver Spring, the six of them: her, Deonte, Malik, Joanna and the children. *Oh, goody.* Joanna and Malik would not let her, or Deonte for that matter, alone with the children. That is, Joanna and Malik had never offered. Lena certainly had not asked. Too afraid of the questions the children might ask. She wondered if Deonte had asked. Probably not. He seemed more uncomfortable around them than Lena did. But he had never lost touch with them. The kids had had Deonte, had known Deonte, all their lives. Lena was someone who disappeared when the kids were two years old, only to resurface when they were ten.

Lena willed Nakeem Joseph and Aron Michelle out of her mind. Right now, she needed an orgasm. It would release sleep chemicals. Sleep hormones. Endorphins. Whatever. She had not tried to masturbate since her mother's wreck. Had been nowhere near the proper mindset.

She thought she was ready now.

Lena was in the mood for something quick — five minutes or less. Using her fingers would take longer, especially since she was, for all intents and purposes, one-handed. Sometimes she liked to use a couple of fingers from both hands to rub together the lips of her vagina. That movement stimulated her clit pretty well, indirectly. Wasn't gonna happen with the cast, so Lena got her vibrator. It looked more like a toy than a vibrator. It was a cute little baker man, complete with painted-on black moustache. It had come with a baker's billowy cap to conceal its extra-long head.

She twisted the bottom — the baker's shoes — and lowered his head to her clit. *Ahh. Yes.* Lena arched her back. *ComeonComeonComeon…*

Mom's in a coma. Lena saw the labyrinth on her mother's head. *What if — shit.* Lena twisted the vibrator off. She took a few deep breaths, trying to clear her mind.

Caris popped into her head. *No. No.* Lena had fantasized about Caris several times during masturbation. Okay, more than several times. And a few times during sex with Caroline.

Caris would get this orgasm done. Easily. But…

Lena gritted her teeth. She *really* wanted to sleep. She closed her eyes and lowered the baker's head to her pussy again. She imagined Caris mounting her. Caris looking down at her with that little lopsided smile.

Caris soft and womanly and saying: "You're crazy hot, Lena. I want to fuck you all night."

Lena kissing her neck.

Caris's breasts. Breasts Lena had actually witnessed. Who cared if the nipples were extra big? That was temporary, and even if it wasn't temporary, Caris was so — she was Caris. Simple. Okay, yeah. Lena pressed the baker's head down harder. She placed herself back in the bathroom. She was on the edge of the tub again, and Caris was on the toilet. Caris wore that nifty bra that exposed her breasts.

"Kiss me," Caris said, so Lena did, and they lived that magical kiss again.

There it was. The orgasm. Quick. Small. Enough to get the job done. Maybe now Lena could sleep.

*****

Caris began practicing in front of the mirror. She would smile, more of a beam, really, and say: "Hello! How nice to see you again. I'd like you to meet Dale, my husband."

Husband.

Husband.

The word did not feel too bad on her tongue, but she was alone. If she said it to a real person…who knew.

It felt wrong when she rocked Donovan and said: "Your father."

Your father.

Your father.

Dale is your father.

That did not feel right.

Caris had to admit she knew next to nothing about transsexualism. She did not have transgender friends. She did know that it was easier to go from male to female because constructing a vagina and clitoris out of a penis was much simpler than making a penis out of a vagina.

Google was her friend. Caris typed the search words "transgender female to male." She clicked on a few random links until she got to TSFAQ.info. One section discussed common reactions and feelings about transition, such as the transgenders' loved ones being fearful the people's inner core would change, that they would become like strangers, that their body changes amounted to mutilation, that they, the loved ones, would never be able to let go of their preconceived idea of the people being a certain sex.

Dale had been nowhere near the point of transition. Nowhere damn near.

Caris worked on a reply to Lena's letter, their kiss humming in her mind all the while.

Lena:
You know how windows get when it rains hard? The rain drills down, the water runs together, and if you look outside, all you see are big blurs. Especially when you're driving. Smudges of red, blue, patriotic smears like it's the Fourth of July, or whatever.

I went to church with your grandmother last Sunday. I'm not religious, but she wanted to go. She's getting to be a foxhole believer. Anyway, so we went to a Methodist church. Shirley went straight to the altar and kneeled. I was more roundabout. I ran my hands over the columns. They were rough. I liked them. They reminded me of your cast. Which I forgot to sign, by the way.

Anyway, once the service started, Shirley was all cocked ears and vigorous, agreeable nods. The pastor had a unibrow. A unibrow. I could not focus on anything except his black fluffy caterpillar, waving, weaving and straining with the fury of the Lord. The pastor caught me gawking. Several times. So I looked at the one stained-glass window. Rain pounded the window, and the angel was a blur. That's not supposed to happen. Rain isn't supposed to change the image in stained glass. Right?

I blinked, and the angel took the shape of a monster—dark, menacing, leering, pointed teeth. My pulse shot up, but when I looked again, the angel was back. Shirley and I drove home in a monsoon. I saw the monster in every blur. That's my life. No definition. A blur. Faint edges. I'm floating, like Dale is. I don't know if I like being a mother. I don't know where I'm going. I'm doing a temporary job soon, though. Three weeks. It'll be nice to get out of the house again and have a life again for a bit.

Anyway, not sure the point of this letter. No need to reply. I hope you're well.
-Caris

*****

Dinner at Applebee's with the Soundros family went okay. Same as usual. Lots of fake smiles and fake laughing from Malik and Joanna. Lots of stolen glances toward Lena and Deonte from Nakeem and Aron. The six of them got together maybe three, four times a year. These dinners lasted an hour, not much more.

This dinner was no different. Nakeem and Aron caught Lena and Deonte up on their friends, activities and grades. Malik and Joanna were great parents. The kids were great kids. They had perfect lives.

Deonte announced that he was engaged. He showed around cellphone pictures of his fiancee. He invited the Soundroses and Lena to the wedding.

Like with the other dinners, Lena left after giving each person a perfunctory hug and feeling as if most of her soul had been scythed out. She loved these children and sometimes even allowed herself the pleasure of referring to them as *her* children. However, she had never been alone with them. Had never had a deep, non-superficial conversation with them. She was glad they were happy and would have it no other way. But, damn. Having them in her life was painful. Sometimes she regretted the open adoption, at least where she was concerned. The kids liked it. They liked knowing their biological mother and father.

Lena hoped Malik and Joanna talked to the children about safe sex. Using condoms. All that jazz. She had been stupid. Hell, she was twenty-nine and still stupid. The children weren't stupid, though. Nope, they were brilliant and lovely.

*****

The third floor of a modest ten-story building in Arlington housed the offices of Gunter & Philpott. Caris entered hesitantly, wondering what to expect. Her life was about to change, again.

The law firm was relatively small, employing five lawyers, three paralegals and seven secretaries/assistants. Caris's new boss was Ted Gunter, a former subordinate of Dale's. Caris glued on a smile and kept her head high as she walked to her desk. People grinned. Some went up to her and introduced themselves. No one seemed to know about Dale. Caris had specifically asked Ted not to say anything. She did not want whispers and furtive, apologetic glances behind her back.

At noon, she joined a group of secretaries from throughout the building for lunch. Several of the women complained about their boyfriends or husbands.

He leaves his underwear on the floor.

He leaves the toilet seat up.

He'd rather watch football than make love.

He goes golfing all weekend and leaves me with the kids.

Caris said nothing. What could she add? *My wife got in a wreck, on purpose, she was a man, I don't know if she's alive or dead, and she left me with a newborn. And I had the most fantastic, most incredible kiss with my stepdaughter. I want more. More, more, more.*

"You're not married?" one of the secretaries or glorified assistants asked, glancing at Caris's bare fingers.

Husband.

I'd like you to meet Dale, my husband.

Caris's stomach constricted with the knowledge of what she was about to say. "Actually, I am. I'm a lucky woman."

The other women leaned in, their expressions expectant. Caris brushed away her apprehension. "My...my..." *My wife.* "My husband," Caris said, the word sour on her tongue, like it had never been before in private, "his name is Dale." *My husband. See, I can do it. See, Dale.* But even as she said the word, thought the word, she knew it was wrong. Felt wrong. She wanted a woman, not a man. "My husband cooks. He does laundry. We have a baby. Dale's great with the baby. He gets up in the middle of the night to help."

Murmurs of admiration and jealousy rippled through the circle at the table. Caris continued speaking, talking about how Dale loved to sing "Twinkle Twinkle Little Star" to Donovan. The lies came quickly and easily. At one p.m., the group headed back to work. No one walked with Caris. Undoubtedly they were weary of hearing about her saintly husband.

*****

Caris brought Donovan for dinner at her mother's house that night. She and Phyllis had chicken, mashed potatoes and biscuits from KFC. Caris nibbled on a plump leg, the lines from earlier at work continuing to zigzag in her mind.

He leaves his underwear on the floor.

He leaves the toilet seat up.

He'd rather watch football than make love.

He goes golfing all weekend and leaves me with the kids.

"Penny for your thoughts," Phyllis said.

Caris scooped mashed potatoes onto a biscuit. She added gravy. *I wonder what Lena's children look like.*

"Tell me about your first day at work," Phyllis prodded.

"It was good. Everyone's nice. I mostly typed and answered phones."

"What'd they say about—you know—about Dale?"

Caris pushed her chair back and got to her feet. "Excuse me. If I go out for an hour, will you watch Donovan?"

Chapter 8

Every table in Azizi was occupied for happy hour and dinner rush, and so were all of the bar stools save two. Most of the clientele were slouched, beaten-down men in business suits. Two waitresses roamed the floor, and Lena was behind the bar. Her hair was down; she still had the cast on. She chatted with a customer, a paunchy, balding man. Lena leaned into him, just a *leeeetle* too much, batting her eyelashes just a *leeeetle* too much. The customer lapped it up.

Yes, Lena was good at her job. Lena would not judge her, would not pester her with questions she did not want to answer. Would understand why Caris said she had a husband.

Lena looked up, met Caris's eyes, and the bar's hustle and bustle faded away. Caris tried to ignore the rush of pleasure in Lena's grin and the shivers of her own body. A momentary panic seized her. She had not realized how much she wanted to be here until she saw Lena.

Caris tried to cover it up as she sat at the bar. "Coke," she said briskly. "Only Coke. Well, a little vodka, too. Vodka and Coke. Can't stay long. I have to get back to the baby."

Lena offered a soft smile. "Of course. I'll take a break soon."

Caris had to look away. Lena's cleavage was visible. Barely. But enough to get Caris's pussy stirring. "Left my horse at home," Caris said. "My revolver, too."

"Yeah. It's not Paris or London, but it's something."

Azizi was little more than a shack, hidden away among the modernity and sameness of Safeway, Chili's Bar & Grill, Panera Bread and Starbucks. The interior was dusty and grimy, like an Old West saloon. Caris liked it. "How do you mix drinks with your cast?"

Lena started on Caris's drink. "Watch me. Slowly. Very slowly. And one-handed, mostly. It's good for business. My tips are up. Too bad I didn't break both arms. I'd be a millionaire."

"That is indeed unfortunate," Caris said.

"Amos." The man across from Caris, the customer Lena had been flirting with, held out his hand.

She shook it. "Caris."

Amos patted his generous belly. "Courtesy of Lena and Azizi."

Caris patted her own belly. "Courtesy of a sperm donor. And going away soon, I hope. Bit by bit."

"Caris is my stepmother," Lena added.

Stepmother. Caris felt old. Very old.

"Stepmother, hey? Cool." Amos's breath was sour, and Caris edged back. "Sorry about your wife."

"Thank you."

"Is drinking all right with your breastfeeding?" Lena asked. "You're still breastfeeding?"

"Yes. I'm trying to go off, but it's taking longer than I hoped. Donovan likes it, and it's supposed to be better than formula. You want a piece of interesting trivia?"

"Sure."

"Alcohol doesn't stay in breast milk. It's like alcohol in blood. Once it's gone, it's gone. So I can still pump and keep milk. Just have to give the alcohol time to go away."

Lena grinned. "I think I'd be too nervous to keep it."

"Me too." Caris took her first sip. The alcohol tingled down her throat and burned her stomach. Caris gulped down a second, more expansive sip. "This is good. I haven't had a drink in close to a year."

"Drink for you here anytime you want one. Hey, be right back." Lena went down the bar to wait on a group of newcomers. She smiled widely, her eyes shining. She touched one of the men lightly, flirtatiously, on the arm, and said: "Hey, guys, let's see some ID, please."

Lucky guy.

"Sorry about your wife," Amos repeated.

"Thank you."

"She still in the coma?"

"Yep."

"She used to come in here a lot. She was nice. Ordered water. Maybe Diet Coke once in a while."

"Yep, she didn't like to drink alcohol." *Was she afraid alcohol would loosen her tongue?*

*****

When Lena's break arrived, they sat on a bench in front of Chili's. "Is this the same bench where your mother told you she was transgender?" Caris asked.

"Yes."

Lena's body against hers was warm, and Caris had to make a conscious effort not to sink into the touch. "I replied to your letter today," Lena said. "Put it in the mail."

"You didn't have to."

Lena shrugged. "Did you go to church with Grandma again?"

"Yes. She likes having someone with her, and it gets me out of the house."

Lena scratched her nose. "So, uh, did you start work yet? That temp job?"

"Today. Actually that's why I'm here. Kind of."

"What happened?"

"I didn't tell anyone there about your mother, the transgender thing, the coma."

Lena nodded. "I don't blame you. I don't tell, either. People treat you differently."

"Ted does, that's for sure. My boss. He kept telling me to leave early and that it's okay take long lunches to visit her. I won't complain. Ted lets me show up at work looking like this." Caris indicated her battle-weary features. "The first face the clients see is someone who should work for Ghoul & Associates." Lena laughed, and Caris smiled, enjoying the sound and Lena's straight, white teeth. "I did something today I probably shouldn't have."

"It's okay to toilet paper the boss' office."

"Of course. I did something else, though."

"What?"

"The women—secretaries or whatever from the building—asked me if I was married. I said yes. I said I had a husband. Husband. Ugh. I would have tried to understand. I really would have."

"I know you would have," Lena whispered.

"But I probably…I don't want a husband. I told them that my husband cooks. Cleans. Does laundry. Helps me with the baby. I didn't plan to lie. Not to that extent, anyway. It squished — squicked — out. I think that's why your mother couldn't tell me. Because she knew deep down inside, I could try to understand all I wanted, but in the end, a man wasn't who I wanted. She knew we were done either way."

Lena's expression was troubled. Contemplative. Her mouth was pink and shone with gloss. Full, enticing lips.

"Does that make you think less of me?"

"No," Lena said in a rush. "Of course not. I don't want a man, either. Mom should have transitioned long ago and met someone in the body that fit him."

Caris sighed. *Find a distraction.* She dared not ask about Lena's children. She glanced toward Chili's. "I did some waitressing in college. Saw lots of families. Smiling. Laughing. There were couples who didn't talk to each other. Couples of all ages and colors. Some weren't even couples, but mother and son, or father and son. Whatever. They sat, drank, ate, maybe said something once in a while such as: 'Oh, it might rain tomorrow,' or 'You have that hair appointment tomorrow, don't you?' "

"I know what you mean."

"Are these types of people happy or sad? Happy they are so comfortable with each other they don't need to talk, or sad that they have nothing to say to each other? That their life together is nothing anymore?"

"I hate to do this, but I have to get back to work. We're really busy. But stay awhile. Please. I'll comp you another drink. Or food. Anything you want."

"No, that's okay. Gotta get back. Thanks for taking the time you did."

They walked to Caris's car, and Caris asked: "Do you miss your mother?"

Lena bit her lip. "Sometimes. Probably not as much as I should."

"It wasn't right of her to do all this to you. The note."

"Hey, would you like to have lunch with me and Karl soon? Or dinner. Or coffee. Or nothing. Just a chat. Maybe talking with Karl would, uh…would help you."

"Karl, huh? Okay. Starbucks this weekend? I might have to bring the baby."

"No problem. Sounds good. I'll let you know what time."

Caris wondered if she should hold out her hand for a handshake goodbye. Or attempt a hug? She and Lena had held up well tonight. No awkwardness, no weird exchanges. Best not to ruin that. But Caris remembered Lena looking at her breasts, these amazed eyes, that kiss. Caris's heart went *thump-thump-thump*.

Lena's gaze was hesitant, yet alert. Indifferent too, or trying to be. Caris wet her lips. *Do you still want to touch my breasts?* She and Lena could have a fling. Why not? A harmless little fling. Lena was not in love with her. Lena barely knew her. So a harmless little—Caris's throat closed up. What the hell was she thinking? *No fling, no fling.* Caris was done with Dale, but that did not mean lusting after Lena was okay. Besides, the fact was that the kiss *had* come from somewhere. Lena must have feelings for Caris, and Caris would not play with them.

But the kiss. The damn kiss was playing games with Caris's mind. Her heart.

"Gotta go," Lena said.

"Can I ask you something?"

Lena shuffled her feet. "You probably shouldn't."

Caris swallowed. "Okay. Good night." She told herself a good night kiss would be okay. On the cheek, of course. Caris leaned in, and the kiss was no more than a brush, a nothing, really, but *damn*. Lena smelled good. Felt good. Tasted good. And then Lena kissed her back, on her cheek.

"Good night," Lena said.

Chapter 9

"Hey, Mom," Lena said on a Thursday a few weeks later. She would be meeting Caris that Saturday at Starbucks; Karl had not been available the past couple of weekends.

No reply from Dale.

Lena took a seat at her mother's bedside. They were alone. "My class was cancelled, so I'm celebrating by coming to see you. How'd you make it this far, huh? Damn."

Nothing.

Lena wriggled the fingers on her left hand. "All free!" Her cast had come off a few days ago, and her left arm was a bit paler than her right. "Not feeling chatty, Mom? Good thing I brought my textbook." Lena had fifty pages to read.

Nothing.

Lena surveyed the tubes going into her mother. Pitiful. Nurses rushed past the door. Someone coding? Dying?

"I told her," Lena whispered. "That you're transgender. Did your dirty work for you."

Oh, she imagined Dale saying.

"She took it fairly well. She, uh, she would've tried to understand. She might even have stayed with…she's great, Mom. You screwed up."

Lena imagined Dale closing her eyes. *I know.*

"Anyway. I haven't cried yet. I wonder what that says about me. What do you think? Am I emotionally stunted? Okay, well. You're stuck listening to me read. No Agatha, sorry. Last chance to speak up. No objections? Okay."

Lena opened her textbook. "The normal distribution was discovered in 1733 by the Hugueneot refugee Abraham de Moivre as an approximation to the binomial distribution when the number of trials is large."

Zzzzz.

Lena retrieved another item of reading material: a letter from Caris, which had arrived earlier that day. "Hey, Mom. Want to help me reply to this letter?"

Dale's lips were set in a thin line.

"You want me to read it to you? Okay, then."

Lena:

You know that many constellations don't look like what they're supposed to, right? (Except the dippers. A square and a handle forming a spoon, I can see that.) But Leo? Do you know that one?

"No," Lena said to her mother. "I hadn't. I looked it up online."

It's supposed to be a lion. It's actually a triangle and a bent clothes hanger. Look up a picture if you don't know what it looks like. Some people reach for explanations. They have to see something with meaning. Anyway, I'm going to see you Saturday, so I'm not writing much. Getting snail mail is nice, isn't it though? Well, I'll see you soon.
     - Caris

"What do you think, Mom?" Lena asked. "You always wanted us to get along." *But not like this, I bet.*

*****

The Starbucks was lively when Caris entered, and she did not see Lena right away. Then there Lena was, wearing her green skirt. She stood by a window table and waved Caris over. A man also stood to greet Caris. He was bespectacled, and his black hair was closely cropped. He was lean and tanned, and stubble dotted his jaws. He was one of the most handsome men Caris had laid eyes on. "Karl Coventry," he said, and extended his hand. Deep, masculine voice.
     "Caris." They shook hands.
     "I'll get our drinks," Lena said. "What do you want?"
     "Hey, congratulations. Your cast is off."
     "Ta-da!" Lena said with a grin.
     Once Lena was gone, Karl proffered a Snickers bar, adorned with a red ribbon. "Dale told me Snickers is your favorite."
     Caris could not help but smile. When she and Dale were first dating, Dale would bring her Snickers bars with red ribbons. So — Dale had cared enough to tell Karl. "Thank you," Caris said. "You want half?"
     A broad grin. "Brought my own. Several, actually." He reached into his messenger bag and sprinkled ten bars, of various permutations — almond, peanut butter, and such — on the table. "I remembered Snickers was your favorite because it's my husband's favorite, too."
     "How did you meet Lena?"
     "We met two years ago in class. I hit on her. She laughed and said no

—
59

way, she only liked the fairer type. We became fast friends."

What about your husband?

Karl nodded, as if Caris had spoken aloud. "Damien and I have an open marriage. We married thirty years ago, long before I accepted I was a man."

Caris nibbled on her bar. Her routine was to eat the top chocolate layer first, then the chocolate on the sides, then the peanut and caramel layer, and finally the nougat and bottom chocolate layer. "So your husband stayed with you."

"We had a rough couple of years, but we worked it out. I was forty-four when I told him and our kids. I was forty-five when I started hormones. Forty-six when I had the surgeries. So, I've been Karl for ten years." He smiled. "Never been happier."

"You look forty. At the most."

Karl bit off a big chunk of Snickers. "I know! It's fantastic."

"Were your kids okay?"

"Pretty much. Damien and I played it cool. If we didn't make a huge deal out of it, the kids wouldn't think it was a huge deal."

"It was sweet of Lena to set this up."

Karl nodded. "I'm lucky she turned me down. I wouldn't trade our friendship for anything."

"I can imagine."

"Dale talked about you a lot."

"How did you meet Dale?"

"Lena and I were partners for a complicated project on taxes. Lena said her mom was a tax attorney and could help us. And she did, a lot. I took Dale out to a thank-you lunch, and Damien came. Lena too."

Caris continued eating the Snickers. She vaguely remembered Dale mentioning the project.

"After lunch, Dale told Lena that Damien didn't seem gay." Karl chuckled. "Whatever gay seems like. Lena told Dale the whole sordid story, that Damien was a straight man married to a transgender. Fine with me. I don't hide I used to be a woman. My past is part of who I am."

"Dale should have told me. I would have tried to understand."

"You're right. He should have."

"He."

A grin. "He. Yeah."

"Why didn't she tell—" Caris stopped. She swallowed, the pronoun *he* a blister on her tongue. "Why didn't he tell me?"

"He'd rejected himself. You'd reject him, too. Or so he thought."

*****

—

60

Lena was glad she had set up a meeting with Karl. He and Caris talked easily, and three was definitely not a crowd. Lena, Caris and Karl chatted for an hour. Not about Dale, though. They talked about Lena's and Karl's MBA program, sports and politics.

At five o'clock, Karl got up to meet his family for dinner. "Karl's nice," Caris said after he left.

Lena replied with a small smile. Caris was sitting next to her; Karl had been across from them.

"You and Karl interact like a couple who has been together forever."

"We do?"

"Oh, yeah." Caris grinned. "You finish each other's sentences. You squabble. It's cute."

"Thanks. I think." Caris was lovely today. Okay, hell, she was lovely every day, and Lena had struggled the past hour not to look overlong at her. Caris had laughed a lot with Karl, and by default, with Lena too. Her eyes shone in a way Lena had not noticed until Caris visited her at Azizi. Caris looked at Lena differently these days. Lena *existed* for her now. That was not to say that when Dale had been up and around, Caris did not realize Lena was attractive. This, though...this was different. Before the kiss, Caris had not been interested in Lena as a woman, as anyone more than her wife's daughter.

Lena hoped she had not opened a can of worms with the kiss. Bad enough that she had to pine after Caris. She did not want Caris pining for her, too. Why did the kiss have to be so good? So incredible, so perfect? *It means nothing, just that the both of us are really good kissers.*

"Does Karl have a penis?" Caris asked.

"N-no. Some do, but the surgery isn't quite there yet, especially to retain sensation. Maybe later."

"It's good to see you again," Caris said.

"Yeah?"

"Yeah. I forgot to tell you this. Remember what you said about cows? Their eyes? I've been looking at pictures of cows. They're calming. You're right. Did you ever put a cow picture up?"

"Mmm."

"Is that a yes?"

"Yes. It's a yes."

Caris laughed. "Did you really?"

"Yep, I really, truly did. I said I would, didn't I?"

"Could I come see it?"

Lena swallowed. "You can, sure. Or, uh...I took a picture of it." Lena pressed a few buttons on her phone. "There."

The picture was black and white, to match the other bathroom pictures. The cow's head was half cocked. "Very cute." Caris gave the phone back. "Will you forward the picture to me?"

Lena fiddled with a few more buttons. "Done."

"Thank you." Caris gave an uneasy grin. She did not ask why Lena had taken a picture of a picture. She probably suspected Lena was scared. And that Lena did not trust herself. Because she sure as hell did not, especially if Caris touched her first. If Caris went in for another hug...oh boy. Lena was not sure how she had managed to limit her response to Caris's cheek kiss at Azizi to another cheek kiss.

Now, it would be so easy for Lena to put her hand on Caris's knee, lean over and — *shit*. Lena's brain felt like a crinkly old map. Handled and folded so many times it was faded and useless. She needed to stop overthinking the situation.

"Nothing happened," Lena said.

Caris licked her lips. "You mean the, uh, the thing in your kitchen?"

"It didn't happen."

Caris crumpled her Snickers wrapper. It had lain untouched for the past hour. "Okay," Caris said slowly. "It didn't happen."

"Right. Didn't happen." What Lena wanted was a do-over. If she and Caris had a do-over, they could make the second kiss bad and sloppy and monstrous, and presto! Problem solved.

Not really. A do-over would make matters worse. The do-over would probably be two times better than the original. A do-over would wreck them, and Caris deserved better.

Aw, hell. Maybe a do-over would not be so bad.

Crinkle crinkle crinkle went Caris's hand with the wrapper, and Lena pressed her hand over Caris's, steadying it. Kisses were not what Caris needed right now. What she needed was a friend. "Caris, I, uh, look, okay. I have cards. Want to play a few rounds? Crazy Eights?" The two of them would be okay. They would be fine; they had no choice.

"Okay," Caris said. "Cards." But she made no move to separate their hands, and neither did Lena.

Chapter 10

Caris had nothing against parades. The St. Patrick's Day parades were the best. They were not as showy or as glittery as the Thanksgiving and Christmas parades and did not take themselves seriously. People cheered loudly for Democratic and Republican politicians alike.

The parade of doctors about eight weeks after the car crash reminded Caris of a parade staple, the clowns who fit into tiny cars, doctor-clowns with long faces and exaggerated frowns. The grave doctor-clowns showed Caris and the rest of the family brain scan after brain scan and explained that Dale's brain stem was fine — but there was no cortical activity. Nothing was happening in Dale's brain. Nothing *could* happen. The doctors liked to talk, their voices low, somber and all-knowing.

Dale was in what doctors suspected was a vegetative state. Dale was operating solely because of her automatic body functions. Only a feeding tube was keeping her alive.

The doctors blathered lots of information and handed over stacks of papers filled with "facts" and statistics. Shirley found her own doctors. They said the same things.

Caris memorized the basics:

— Most persistent vegetative state patients have no perception of external stimuli and cannot respond to such stimuli.

— Any movement or seeming response to external stimuli is purely coincidental. Don't look for patterns. They're not there.

— PVS patients have normal sleep-wake cycles. They are capable of moving their limbs, although only as a reflex. They can open their eyes and smile. It may seem like they are tracking objects or people with their eyes. Don't delude yourself. They're not looking at shit.

— PVS patients cry, laugh, groan, moan, scream and make a whole host of noises. They ain't feeling or saying shit.

— Most PVS patients cannot chew or swallow food. They require feeding tubes.

— The feeding tube is usually the only life-sustaining piece of equipment necessary, as PVS patients can breathe on their own and their brainstems are relatively fine.

— It costs about $250,000 a year to care for someone in a PVS. The first few years of care are the most expensive, sometimes running into the millions per year.

— Life expectancy for PVS patients depends in part on why they are in the PVS. If it is because of a traumatic brain injury, the life expectancy is generally higher, although paralysis often accompanies traumatic brain injury. The life expectancy prognosis is bleaker if the cause is lack of oxygen to the brain.

— Survival more than ten years is rare. The cause of the vegetative state itself is often the cause of death. Other big reasons for the short life expectancy are complications such as secondary infections (pneumonia), urinary tract infections, pulmonary tract infections, general system failure, strokes or tumors.

— No treatment or cure exists.

What gave Shirley optimism:

— If PVS patients do wake up, they are more likely to do so during the first month—and without warning.

— There is controversy over consciousness in PVS. Some PVS patients, as many as forty percent, may be misdiagnosed. They are actually minimally conscious and capable of meaningful activity, such as tracking objects purposefully and slightly moving their hands.

And the grimmest facts of them all:

— If patients do not emerge within the first year, they probably never will. If, somehow, they do emerge after the first year, they are very likely to have severe disabilities.

— The younger and healthier the patient is, the longer she should live.

Dale was neither of these things. She was fifty-six years old and had been at least thirty pounds overweight before the crash. Thank goodness Shirley had money. Dale's insurance did not cover everything.

Dale had left a living will, dated about three years prior to the car wreck. Caris had one, too. Benefits of being married to a fussy lawyer. Their living wills gave each other authorization to make medical decisions on the other's behalf. One of the first things most living wills dealt with were conditions such as persistent vegetative states, and Dale's living will was no different. Dale stated that in such a case, she would want treatment, meaning life-prolonging measures, such as the feeding tube, for one year. If there was little or no progress after the year, Dale wanted the tube pulled.

Fairly clear. No mention of what to do in cases of paralysis, though. The paralysis would compromise Dale's quality of life greatly if she were to emerge from the PVS. Caris was not sure Dale would have wanted that—depending on other people for such basic needs as the toilet, for example. Peeing and shitting in her bed.

Shirley was buoyant. Science was making leaps and bounds. Stem cells were marvels. And with therapy, quite a few paralyzed people walked again. Caris could sense Shirley maneuvering behind the scenes, setting up grounds to challenge the living will if Dale remained in the PVS come April.

Lena was a shadowy presence. She showed up for every meeting with the doctors but said little. She usually sat across from Caris, and sometimes Caris would study her, her eyes, brown or green, her pinched lips, her unreadable expression, and wonder what she was thinking. Lena was lovely in her own distant, closed-off way. More lovely, more beautiful than Dale. Sometimes Lena would meet Caris's gaze, and neither of them would break the eye contact right away. Caris would remember how they had been at Starbucks, just sitting there, Caris's hand beneath Lena's, them just sitting, doing nothing, just enjoying the feel of each other.

*****

Caris got a letter from Lena, through postal mail. This one did not have a salutation. It read:

REGINALD PHILIP ISMAY, reads my father's grave marker. Have you been to where he is buried? Goodacres Memorial Gardens in Arlington. I hate the name. Goodacres? Gardens? Okay. Okaaay. I visit once a year, on the anniversary of his death.

So of course I went last week. I usually go in the evenings when it is cooler, so I can stay a while. Mom used to go in the mornings and leave a rose. So, imagine my shock when I went last week and there was a rose.

You left it, didn't you? (Or maybe Grandma or Granddad did.) Did Mom take you to her first husband's grave? I'm not sure if that's romantic or creepy. It's both, I suppose.

So, there is a space next to Dad's plot. For Mom, of course. Mom never told me much about him. She said it hurt her too much. Oh, she told me the basics—what I call questionnaire information. Not the important stuff—what made him laugh? What made him sad? She talked about that stuff only a few times. I don't have a single memory of him.

Maybe this sounds awful, but this vegetative state thing? Mom is in there, laughing her lily white coma ass off at us, pointing fingers at us. She'll come out when she's damn well ready and wants to. When she's made us suffer enough. All she did was lie and manipulate. I'm done with her bullshit. That's what I think some days.

The real situation, though, is that she would not want this. She's gone. She's dead. Grandma is deluding herself. Do you buy that stuff Grandma says? About science, how in a year or five years, we never know what medicines there will be, medicines better than Zolpdiem. The study that says forty-seven of sixty-five patients with locked-in syndrome indicated they were happy? I read that study. It had lots of holes.

Whenever I touch Mom, she is so dry and brittle that I half-expect her face to crumble. Her eyes are doll eyes. Mannequin eyes. It's a shame. I wish she wouldn't have done this. She didn't have to try to kill herself. By a year Grandma will have Mom on Zolpidem and other medications and deep brain stimulation and God knows what else, and she'll try to coax more time out of you. Maybe you'll give it. I kind of hope you do. I don't want my mother to die. Even though she is already dead.

Karl and I went out to Klondike last weekend. My sole Saturday night off this month. It's a gay club in DC. He got me drunk (okay, I helped get myself drunk, too) and I ended up making out with a few random women. Hell if I remember their names or what they looked like. I've stayed away from Caroline. Don't worry.

Hope all is well with you. Have you been back to Dr. Frowny Face? I hope you're enjoying Donovan now. I'll come by to visit him sometime soon. Promise. Well, hey, I guess I'll see him at the birthday party this Sunday. Gotta love Grandma, huh? See you soon.

- Lena

Chapter 11

Dale turned fifty-seven years old three months after the wreck. Lena entered the hospital, her stomach like a rock. Shirley was throwing a birthday party. "Just a little something with cake," Shirley had said on the phone, but Lena wondered. She wanted to turn around and drive away. *Cough cough. Coming down with something nasty.*

A birthday party, really? Lena hoped it would not be an awkward, overboard shebang with balloons and streamers, apparent gaiety with her mother's lifeless form in the midst. Shirley had the tendency to overshoot sometimes.

Don't be such a Sour Sally. Might do you good to celebrate.

Lena got on the elevator. She was one to talk about balloons. She had brought two. Yep, two balloons. To this fake-a-roo birthday party. Granted, they were little helium birthday balloons on sticks in a vase.

Still, they were balloons.

She did not feel right showing up empty handed. Shirley and George were bringing cake. Caris was bringing drinks.

Lena: nothing.

So she'd stopped at Safeway for a quick card. Only it hadn't been so quick. All the cards seemed in bad taste, considering her mother's situation.

Balloons it was, then. One was blue, her mother's favorite color, and read HAPPY. The other was green and read BIRTHDAY!

Lena's grandparents, Caris and Donovan were in the room, and Shirley squealed. "Perfect! George, see. Lena brought balloons. I was telling your grandfather we needed to dress this party up."

Shirley set the vase holding the balloons next to the cake. "Chocolate cake," Shirley explained with a beam. "Your mother's favorite."

Lena ventured a smile at Caris, and Caris smiled back. A few seconds longer than necessary. Maybe more than a few seconds longer.

George cut the cake. It had white frosting and read HAPPY BIRTHDAY in blue letters. The cake was good. Moist, not too sweet, and Caris whispered to Lena that she would have a letter arriving in the mail probably Monday. Weird relationship they had, but given the situation and who they were to each other, it worked.

The party progressed better than Lena thought it would. No singing "Happy birthday." No forced joviality. Just cake, drinks and chatting. Reminiscing. But Dale was in a wheelchair, on the outskirts of their chatter.

With these eyes. These awful dead glassy eyes absorbing nothing.

Lena's stomach was still a rock.

Shirley, sometimes in a choked-up voice, talked about Dale's past birthdays. Some were stories Lena had heard a million times, but a few were new.

"Last year," George said. "This time last year. Dale came up for the weekend. You remember, Caris? You went to a movie with Shirley. Dale and I went boating, just the two of us. The wind was in her hair. She'd never looked happier." He glanced toward the woman in the wheelchair. "Do you remember, sweetie?"

Donovan cooed.

An exquisite sorrow creased George's face. "Have you cried?" he asked Lena.

"What? Cried? No."

George frowned. "Me either."

"I have," Caris said. "Two or three times but not like I should. If that makes sense. My first night home after having Donovan, I kept waiting for the hospital to call with the news Dale had died. The call never came. When that call comes..." Caris let her voice trail off. "It's the limbo."

"I haven't cried at all," Lena whispered. *Not even about the children.* "What do you think that means?"

"It's the limbo," Caris repeated. "It blankets everything. It's contagious."

"Dale's coming back," Shirley said firmly. "You just wait and see."

"You're delusional," Lena muttered under her breath.

"What?" Shirley asked.

"Nothing, Grandma."

*****

When Lena got home, she called Joanna. "I was hoping I could do something with the kids soon. They'd like that, I think."

"Okay," Joanna replied slowly. "Do you mean just you and the children?"

"Whatever you are comfortable with. You're their mother."

"Right, right," Joanna said. "Well, let me talk to Malik and the kids. I'll get back to you."

"All right," Lena whispered. "Thanks." She hung up and fixed herself a glass of water. Joanna was not going to call back. Wasn't going to talk with Malik and the kids.

Part of Lena was relieved.

*****

Caris had gone through several drafts of her reply to Lena's latest letter. Lena's father, Reggie, and Dale had married in Honolulu, Hawaii, when they were both twenty-six. They were slender and dark. They looked like different sides of the same coin. In the wedding picture, Dale wore a lacy, soft white dress and a purple lei: femininity personified. The modern Dale hated that picture. "I was a sucker for tradition," Dale had said.

Five years after the wedding, Reggie was dead from AIDS, leaving behind Dale and their four-year-old daughter. Reggie was healthy, vital, alive in the wedding album. In subsequent pictures, he was increasingly pale and sickly.

Reggie and Dale had taken a somewhat convoluted path to the altar. They were both young achievers. They became best friends at college, at the University of Virginia, although Reggie was three years behind Dale. It did not matter they were both gay and could not, did not want to, complete the physical component of their relationship with each other. The emotional part was enough. They happily fucked other people but knew they wanted children one day. They wanted the traditional "family life." It was a different, more closeted world back then. They got married and hoped the honeymoon was the only time they would need to have sex with each other. It was — and luckily for Dale and Lena. Otherwise, they might have gotten the virus, too.

Dear Lena, Caris wrote.

Your mother loved your father. To be honest with you, it's one reason I thought your mother and I would have a great marriage. She talked about him like she really, truly loved him. Like he was her soul mate, despite the fact they were both gay. Your mother wouldn't take marrying again lightly, or so I thought. I used to think—and still do—that your mom loved him in every way. But he didn't love her back in the way that counted. Interesting how sexuality works, isn't it? It's possible that for your mother, her first marriage was not one of convenience.

I'm sorry your mother did not tell you much about your dad. She told me some things. I'll write down what I remember. Here's a little something to get you started in case you don't know this already.

Your parents met in class. His handwriting was what drew her to him. They sat together, exchanged hellos, nothing special. Then class began, and your father took notes. His writing was elegant, like calligraphy. Like art. Your mother was mesmerized. That night, they went to a party where he was a drag queen. He wore a sparkly green dress, and his singing voice captivated your mother.

Now, about your mother and her future, I am not challenging the living will. Your mother wanted a year, and I'm giving that year. No more, no less. The paralysis issue troubles me, but I won't presume to read your mother's mind. Your grandmother has a point, however far-fetched. Lena, your mother could recover. Maybe not completely, but meaningfully. She— he—could have good years left. Your mother has two beautiful children whom I know, I absolutely know, he would want to see grow and flourish. Sometimes, I think about how your mother struggled for years. All that agony and torture. Now it's apparently over. Just so sudden. If your mother gets a second chance, I think she will make the most of it.

Lena, your mother loved you so, so much. I wish I could convey how much. She wasn't some villain. But of course you know that.

Do you want my wedding ring and my engagement ring? Sell them or something. Get some cash. I don't want them. Don't know what to do with them. Well, I know what I want to do with them. Flush them down the toilet. But that's a lot of money going down the crapper. Maybe I will save them for Donovan if you don't want them. You're going to ask if your mother and I are done for sure, so here's the answer. Yes, we are. We were over a good while before Donovan was born. Doesn't mean I don't love her. I always will in a way. She was my wife. I hope she wakes up and gets her second chance, but I'm not interested in being part of it. I'm not taking her back in any scenario. I'll be there to help your mother if she wants, but it won't be as her wife. She hurt me too much.

You know what, Lena. I can't call her 'him.' I just can't. Not if your mother didn't have the guts to come to me and tell me. Because otherwise, saying he, his or him feels like a fraud.

Are we going to tell your grandparents that your mother was transgender? Maybe that would only complicate things for them. And maybe someone should still idealize Dale.

But maybe they should know.

It rained when I left the rose at your father's grave. Fat, fast raindrops, but I had an umbrella. I sat and chatted a bit with him. Told him you and I were getting along better.

- Caris

*****

Two weeks later, Shirley settled on a rehabilitation facility and began preparations for Dale's transfer. For Caris, the word Pinewood conjured scents of a Disney lovefest. Pine trees, clear, babbling brooks, fresh air, butterflies, dancing deer, Snow White shitting roses and rainbows. Lurking behind the Disneyfication was reality.

Pinewood was where patients went to drool and whittle away time. Pinewood was where relatives visited every day at first and then later, once a week, if the patient was lucky. Pinewood was as guilt-free a place as any to abandon people to their deaths. However, Dale would not need to worry about abandonment, thanks to her mother. The choice had come down to either the Shepherd Center in Atlanta or Pinewood. Pinewood won because of its proximity. Certainly not because of its costs. It cost about a third more than the Shepherd Center. Shirley did not want Dale to be cared for at home. "My daughter needs to be where nurses and doctors can help at a moment's notice," Shirley stressed.

And so Dale's last night at the hospital had arrived. Tomorrow, Disney World! Pinewood! At least there would not be lines for the rides.

Later that week, George and Shirley were moving into a rental condo down the street from Pinewood. Caris had a hard time believing she had lived with them about four months. *Wow.* In some ways, she felt like they had moved in yesterday. In other ways, she felt like they were old roommates. Once they were out, Caris planned to start packing some of Dale's things. Definitely the bedroom.

She decided to stay with Dale the last night at the hospital, although she was not sure why. Maybe to have a conversation, however one-sided. A conversation about forgiveness. About moving on. Divorce. Dale's future, or lack thereof.

"So, Dale," she said. "About us. We're over, were over before the wreck, but you knew that."

Nothing.

"What do you want, Dale? Do you want to die? Should I push to let you go now?"

Nothing.

Caris tried to sleep on the lumpy cot. She must have succeeded for at least a bit, because she awoke with a start some time later. She checked her cellphone. Eleven-thirty, so the night yawned before her. *Great.* She went to the window. She drew the curtains back and pulled the blinds up. The moon scowled down at her. A sense of foolishness overtook Caris. She had been stupid to expect some sort of closure, some sort of meteor shower that spelled out L-E-T M-E D-I-E or I A-M A-L-I-V-E.

A whisper: "Hey."

Caris whirled around. Lena, bathed in the moon's rays.

"I didn't mean to scare you," her stepdaughter said. "Sorry."

"Lena. Hey. It's okay."

"I couldn't sleep," Lena said. "Figured I'd come here. Maybe I shouldn't have stayed after I saw you asleep, but..." Lena shrugged. "I fell asleep right away in the chair. The hard, un-fucking-comfortable chair."

"Did I wake you up?"

"Yes, but it's fine."

Caris poured herself and Lena small glasses of water. The moon or a cloud shifted, leaving Lena half in shadow. She was eerie, like a shape shifter.

"How's work?" Caris asked. "We haven't talked in a while." That was true. Lena had never replied to Caris's letter.

"Work's good."

"School? You in summer school?"

"Summer school is over. But yeah, school is decent."

Lena obviously was not in a talkative mood, and Caris's shoulders ached. She felt the weight of the day ahead. Tottering mounds of paperwork, the monitoring. The worrying. The wondering. "Well, off I go. You need your time with your mother."

"You stay. You belong in that cot. I don't. But if it's okay with you, I'll stay too. I'll read and nap in the chair or something."

"I don't belong in that cot, Lena. I'm here to try to figure some answers. Make sure what your mother would've wanted. Make sure I'm doing the right thing."

"Still—"

"I'm not letting you bunk in a chair." Caris surveyed the cot. The fit would be doable. But tight. Very tight. Having Lena in bed with her was tempting. Very. Feeling her heat, hearing her breathing, the beat of her heart.

"We're not getting in that cot together," Lena said, her expression unreadable.

"Of course not. I'm going home. The place is all yours. Let's do something soon, though, okay? I've missed you."

"Missed you, too."

Caris slung her purse over her shoulder.

"Are Grandma and Granddad at the townhouse with Donovan?"

"Yep."

"You want the keys to my place? You can stay there and maybe get a good night's sleep."

"I look that bad, huh?"

Lena grinned. "No, no, don't be crazy. It's the least I can do for kicking you out." She slid two keys off her key ring. "So, do you want them? The orange one is for the front door. Blue one for my unit."

In other words, will you stay with me tonight? Was that Lena's true question? No, of course it was not. But Caris found herself whispering: "If you come too. Not that I—well, I just meant—to talk and catch up. If you wanted. Because I have missed you. Well, no. Of course you don't want to. You're staying here. I'm sorry. Yes, thank you. I'll take the keys. I appreciate it."

Lena searched Caris's face a long moment, and Caris wondered if the acknowledgement, understanding and desire on Lena's expression reflected her own. Caris saw fear, too, causing her chest to squeeze. "Never mind," Caris mumbled. "I'm going home. Good seeing you again."

"Caris?"

"What?" *Could my voice be any more choked?*

"Mom never—and you've never mentioned your father. What's up with him?"

She doesn't want me to go. "That's a good question. I never knew who he was. My mother used to say his name was Carl Louis, and that's how I got my name, by combining Carl and Louis."

"You don't believe her?"

"When I was ten, she admitted she had no clue who he was. My mother used to be an alcoholic. She blacked out a lot. Remembered nothing."

"Oh."

Caris laughed, trying to break the awkwardness. "Maybe I'm a long-lost princess. I'm heir to the throne of an obscure European country. Her Royal Highness Caris Ismay. Your mother is the princess now. If only the kiss of love would wake her up."

"Have you tried?"

"Tried what? Kissing her awake? No."

"You going to?"

"No."

Lena went to her mother. She kissed Dale's forehead and both her cheeks. Then her chin. Lena was like a porcelain doll, delicate and fragile, half in moonlight, half in shadow. A porcelain doll who caused Caris's heartbeat to speed up. She imagined Lena was kissing her instead of Dale, and Caris's arms prickled. Her neck longed for Lena's mouth. "Wake up, Mom. We miss you." When Lena returned her focus to Caris, Lena's expression was somber and grave. "What do you think about do-overs?"

"Do-overs? You mean like your mom if she wakes up?"

"Or..." Lena exhaled a heavy sigh. "Yeah, yeah. That's what I meant. Hey, why do you want to go home with me tonight, Caris?"

"Like I said. To catch up." Maybe if Caris said the words enough, they would magically become true.

"To catch up," Lena echoed, and Caris wondered if the factors running through Lena's mind were the same factors that had been whirling through her own the past few weeks. *Could we have a fling and come out of it okay, with no hurt feelings? Without anyone finding out? Without falling in love? What if Dale wakes up? And and and and...*

"All right, Lena whispered. "Let's get out of here."

Chapter 12

Lena got to her apartment first and stayed in her car to wait for Caris. *Great going, Lena.* She should have left the hospital the moment she entered her mother's room and realized Caris was asleep in the cot. And Lena *had* left. Kind of. She had gotten as far as the elevator banks before returning to her mother's room. She'd told herself she was being silly. There was no reason to flee Caris. Caris and Lena were adults.

So, Lena had settled into the chair and...wham.

Caris was spending the night. Not with Dale, but with Lena. Lena was ready to get the agony out of her system. She and Caris needed to fuck, to get the fucking over with, preferably tonight.

Lena drummed her fingers on the steering wheel. Where was Caris? *Bet she's chickening out.*

*****

Caris was lost in thought as she drove. When she got home — and she was going home, she was not going to Lena's, no way — she would...what? Rattle around the darkened living room while George slept? Break out the home movies again, see Dale in her full glory at the beach, skiing, at their wedding? Pray Donovan would not cry? Masturbate? Caris's throat ached. Her pussy hummed hotly. If she masturbated, she would not come easily. Because she would be thinking about Lena.

Lena waiting for her. Lena, abandoned. By Caris. Lena who would never write her a letter again.

Come off it. Nothing's going to happen. She and Lena would talk. And go to sleep. All there was to it. Certainly there would not be sex. Caris had to remember that her pussy was a thorny bramble thicket of weeds. She had not trimmed since Dale's crash. No way was Lena going anywhere near the pussy. Or her breasts.

*****

Lena flicked on the lights to her bedroom, and Caris's gaze fell upon

Diana, Princess of Wales. A cardboard cutout. She turned a questioning look on Lena.

Lena shrugged. "I like the royals."

Her bed was a queen size. The covers were blood red with bands of vertical, thin green and yellow stripes. Her furniture and curtains were light green. The cumulative effect was soothing.

Lena proffered a pair of sweat pants and a Holstein-sized T-shirt. *Not my size anymore*, Caris almost said.

"You change here," Lena remarked. "I'll change in the bathroom."

When Lena emerged from the bathroom, Caris knew getting to sleep would be a problem. Huge problem. *Damn you, Lena.* Sexy, hot Lena, her dark hair shiny, flowing and loose. Sexy, hot Lena wearing smiley face boxer shorts and a tight purple wife beater. These breasts. These long legs. *Is she torturing me on purpose?*

Caris set her phone alarm. "I'm getting up at six. We're moving your mother at eight. You going?"

"I guess, for a bit. Maybe not at six unless — do you want me to keep you company? Why so early?"

"I want to make sure everything goes smoothly. I'll probably have paperwork to sign before she's released from the hospital. Your grandmother's coming, so she can keep me company. You sleep in."

Lena's eyelashes fluttered. "No, I'll, I'll go with you. She's my mother. I should be there." Lena turned off the main light. She tapped on the touch lamp by the bed, and they got into bed. Gingerly, awkwardly.

"You look nice," Caris said.

"I look nice? I'm wearing pajamas."

"Exactly. Have you taken a look lately at yourself in these pajamas?"

Lena pressed a hand to her forehead. "Let's fuck and get it over with. All right?"

Caris laughed, a choking laugh. "I don't want to fuck you if it means not being your friend."

"Are we friends?"

"I think we are. We wouldn't write each other letters if we weren't."

Lena used her elbow to prop her head up. "Good point."

"How are, uh, how are Nakeem and Aron?"

"Fine. I guess." Tight smile.

Caris let her gaze fall to Lena's cleavage. To Lena's full breasts. A jet droned overhead, reminding Caris of Shirley's snores.

Lena let Caris look. Without comment.

Then Lena said: "I usually sleep naked."

"I like sleeping naked. When your grandparents move out Friday, I'm going to close the blinds and have myself and Donovan a naked party."

"Did you and Mom sleep naked?"

"Not usually."

"You think because she didn't like her body? Sleeping naked reminded her she didn't have a penis?"

"Could be."

"This is a weird conversation we're having."

Caris chuckled. "You started it."

"Guilty as charged." Lena gave Caris's shoulder a quick, brisk squeeze. "We should go to sleep. Will you tap the lamp off?"

"Yes." Caris tapped the lamp off. After her eyes adjusted to the dark, she studied the dim outlines of Lena, amazed by her closeness. Her beauty. She wanted to trace the edges of Lena's face, her nose, her lips.

"Are you awake?" Lena asked.

Caris cupped Lena's cheek. "Yes. You want something quick?"

"Just wanted to say thank you for coming over."

"Thank you for letting me."

"I bet you miss this. Being in bed with someone."

"I do," Caris whispered. "But I could get this with other people. That's not why I'm here. You're — you're…never mind."

"When you're ready, maybe you already are ready, you should start dating. See lots of people. Have fun."

"Do you like dating? I'm not crazy about it. It's artificial. Stilted."

"Stilted like us right now? Yeah?"

Caris attempted a playful smile in case Lena could see it in the dark. "Yes."

"You ought to go out with people."

"I will, I will."

"When you smile, do you know one edge tugs up more than the other?"

Caris's stomach became warm and tingly. "You like my smile?"

"It's cute. Nakeem and Aron have that smile, too."

"They do?"

"Mmm."

"Is that why you like me?"

Lena laughed. "Oh, Caris."

Caris's heart went *thump-thump-thump* at the undertone in Lena's laugh. "I'm not going to be able to sleep," Caris said.

"Me either."

Caris's legs were wobbly. Unsteady. Never mind that she was in bed. Her legs had been goners since she realized she was going home with Lena. Caris's body was on fire. She felt eighteen again. She was nervous, horny, fearful, about to melt. She had a burning desire, an aching need, for another meaningful kiss, for true sex, two-way, passionate, hair-pulling, panting, moaning, groaning, sweaty sex. For hours and hours. Not a sterile wham bam, thank you, ma'am. If only her pussy was in shape. If only her breasts were.

Caris's stomach was a mess of somersaults. *Why did I come tonight? Stupid, stupid.*

She and Lena would fuck. Eventually. Sex with Lena. *Oh my God, my God* — anything else than sterility with Lena would be dangerous. Caris would have to find a way to depersonalize their sex experience. Not just because of who Lena was, but also because of Caris's edginess about her baby-changed body. Blows Dale had delivered to her sexual self. Caris was a woman who had not had true sex in close to a year, and Lena was not the person to change that.

A wham bam ma'am was easy. Uncomplicated. Caris would find a way to make *that* happen when she and Lena did fuck. Not lovemaking. No kisses.

"Caris?"

Lena kissed her, a brush of mouth against mouth, and then Caris reached for Lena, for another kiss, slightly longer. Their hips pressed into each other, and then Caris was on top of Lena, and she was kissing Lena's neck. Lena tasted of sweat and *LenaLenaLena*, she was delicious, and Lena moaned, and groaned, and Caris did too, and it was over quickly. All they had to do was rub their pussies against each other. Fastest orgasm Caris had in her life, especially with clothes on. Perfect degree of depersonalization too, but afterward, Lena gathered Caris into her arms, and Caris burrowed into her.

"Bowling tomorrow night?" Lena asked.

"I would love that."

*****

Azizi was mostly full when Caris walked in at seven-fifteen for bowling. Lena had said to come by about seven-thirty. Her shift ended at eight.

Caris locked in on Lena, wiping off a table across the room. For a second, her profile was Dale's, and Caris's chest squeezed. Then Lena looked up, met Caris's eyes, and grinned shyly. Definitely not Dale now; their faces were very different. *Thank God.*

Caris thought she would be okay bowling. She and Lena needed each other. They were in a unique situation and could help each other like no one else could. They could be great friends. They were adults. They would not let silly crushes and physical stuff like the best kiss of Caris's life get in the way.

Lena waved hello. She weaved around tables, until she was with Caris. "Hey, Caris," Lena said, drawing out the name just a little. *Caaaris. Hey, Caaaris.* Or perhaps Caris was imagining it. Lena's hair was in a ponytail, but loose tendrils softened her face. She wore dressy black pants and a silk green shirt that brought out her eyes. Caris was a frump in her maternity jeans and blue top. On purpose, she had not shopped for clothes for this "date," because she had no need to impress Lena. Right? They were not in a relationship nor possibly headed that way; they were passing ships, temporary friends with benefits. They were passing ships not meant to end up together but who came together when the need was there.

"Thanks for letting me crimp your style. Hope you don't mind I'm a little early," Caris said.

"I'm furious. Come on, sit. What can I get you?"

"Vodka and Coke again. Trying to get me drunk so you can beat me at bowling?"

Lena winked. "You know it."

*****

The bowling alley was mostly full. "Let's get your stuff," Lena said. Caris ended up with red and tan clown shoes, with thick black laces. No fair. The shoes Lena brought from home were purple, sleek and attractive.

"If I lose, I'm blaming my shoes. That looks like mold growing on the left one," Caris grumbled.

Lena won the first game, 205 to 135. "You set me up," Caris said accusingly.

Lena laughed. "What?"

"What? What?" Caris mocked Lena. "Two hundred and five? Who bowls that?"

"Someone's competitive."

Caris shook her head. "Two hundred and five! We're going to a movie next time."

Next time.

Lena looked at her, catching the slip, too. "Next time," Lena repeated. "Is that okay?"

"Sure, sure, whatever. I'd like that."

Sometime during the second game, and after they'd had a couple of beers, Caris realized the warm glow inside her was not her mild buzz. It was a glow of fun. *This is what it's like to be out and have fun.* I'd almost forgotten. She had not thought about Dale. Or about herself. Or, amazingly enough, about who Lena was. She lost herself in Lena's laugh, in her brown-green eyes. Caris was merely someone out with a friend and having playful adult conversations. Perfectly ordinary. She liked feeling normal again. No one treating her with kid gloves because of her vegetative wife.

Lena won the second game, 211 to 132. "Best of four," she said with a wink.

Caris took Lena's hand. "Time for *me* to show off. Come on." A jumble of stuffed animals crowded the display at a claw crane game. "See anything you like?"

"These are rip offs. Money vampires."

"I'm pretty good at them."

Lena's brows rose. "Really? Okay. That bowling ball doll is adorable. That's a perfect way to remember tonight."

"You'll want to remember tonight?"

"211 to 132? Gee. Let me think."

Caris swatted Lena's shoulder. "Ugh. You're awful."

Game three also went to Lena, and she and Caris walked out together. Not quite holding hands, but close, hands brushing each other. Lena had put her bowling ball doll prize in her bowling bag. The parking lot lights exposed a sky that was gray, smudgy, polluted. Not exactly beautiful. Caris barely noticed, thanks to the beer tumbling in her veins. The moon was moving. Or maybe that was her newfound heady sensation.

"Want to go somewhere else or call it a night?" Lena asked.

Caris ran her hands over Lena's car, a lime green VW bug. Lena had driven them to the alley. "I told your grandparents I'd be back by ten-thirty to give Donovan his bottle." Caris had set the early deadline as a precaution to avoid getting *too* chummy with Lena. But right now, she was cursing herself.

"It's ten o' clock," Lena said.

"I'll call and see if one of them will do it. I'm sure they will." If Caris went home, Donovan would cry, his wails rising and rising and his lips would pucker for her cow udders and Shirley would be *How did it go with Lena so glad you're becoming friends Tell me everything doesn't she bowl good, that's my granddaughter.* Caris could not wait to have the house to herself.

Caris realized one reason she had enjoyed her time with Lena so much: Caris had come of her own free will, on her own terms. No one pawed at her, needled her insistently, demanded she sacrifice herself for them. Even Dale hovered, silent, waiting. Demanding. But with Lena, Caris found a few hours of peace. Lena asked nothing of her. Lena accepted Caris for who she was.

"Caris? Are you all right? Can I come see the baby?"

Caris's heart lurched. *Lena wants to see the baby?* It's a miracle. Caris grinned, her anxiety floating away. "Definitely."

Chapter 13

They went to Azizi to get Caris's car, then drove separately to the townhouse. The lights were off as Caris and Lena approached the front door. "We'll have to be quiet," Caris said. "Remember your grandfather sleeps downstairs."

"Got it."

Caris inserted her key into the lock. She slipped her hand into Lena's and entwined their fingers. To guide Lena across the darkened room. No other reason. *Riiight.* She loved their hands together. Had kept their hands together as much as possible while they'd been at the claw crane game. Lena certainly had not seemed to mind.

Caris led Lena around a table and to the staircase. She heard a click, and light illuminated the room. "Caris?" George, from the pull-out couch. He had turned on a lamp.

Lena dropped her hand from Caris's. "Hey, Granddad." She went over to hug him. "Now I can see."

"You girls have fun?"

Caris joined them. "Did you know your granddaughter is a professional bowler?"

They made small talk for a few minutes. "Donovan was good tonight," George said.

"He never cries with you or Shirley," Caris agreed. She shifted her gaze to Lena. "Now, me..." She laughed. "My face is a trigger for him to cry."

*****

In the kitchen, Lena watched Caris retrieve a pot and fill it with hot water. Caris also got a full baby bottle from the refrigerator. She put the bottle into the pot. She swirled the bottle around — "to make sure the heat distributes evenly" — and tested a few drops on her forearm. "Warm," she said. "Good."

"Let me feel."

Caris squeezed milk on Lena's arm. The warmth was like soup that had a minute to cool off. "That's a lot of work for a bottle," Lena said.

"It's not too bad. But serves me right for getting a cheap warmer. So, uh, you didn't feed your children?"

Lena ignored the pinprick at her heart. "I didn't. And please don't call them my children. I'm not their mother."

"You love them. I see it when — "

"I've never seen Granddad smile like that."

"Yes," Caris said, and a shadow came into her eyes. "He loves that baby. He could talk about Donovan all day."

"Do you love him?"

"He's my son. Okay, let's go up."

On the way up, Lena daydreamed, imagining what would happen when she and Caris kissed again. *If* they did. What kind of lover was Caris? Tender? Attentive? Playful? Dominant? A combination? What kind of lover was Dale? What kind of kisser? Would Caris compare the two of them? Yes, of course. It was inevitable, and Lena would try not to think about it.

It did not really matter, anyway. Lena doubted she would find out what kind of lover Caris was. Her true lover self, anyway. She and Caris would divert to Plan B.

Plan A: Lovemaking. Taking their time. Gazing into each other's eyes. Exploring. Whispering. Laughing. Definitely doable between good friends, people who had a high attraction to each other and who were looking for a good time and to forget their realities. Would likely not work for her and Caris, because of that perfect kiss and because of their connection.

Plan B: Precious little foreplay, if any. Selfish fucking. Getting off as quickly as possible. Not much touching. Orgasm-oriented. Every woman for herself. Lots of business talk. Talk about work, or shopping, or the nice weather, or the hair appointment tomorrow, like Caris had touched on in front of Chili's.

Plenty of other plans too — all the way to Z. But, yeah, Plan B was where she and Caris were headed.

For the best, really.

It went unsaid that she and Caris would tell no one, absolutely no one, what was happening between them. Lena certainly was not going to tell Karl. Maybe Caris had, or would, tell Jennifer. Whatever Caris needed. *Sucks to be head over heels in love with her.* Lena could do it, of course — could pretend that her feelings for Caris were nowhere near where they really were. She *had* to. Caris was fresh out of a marriage and did not deserve the pressure of being with someone wildly in love with her. Caris needed a friend to help her get back the swing of things, and Lena was fine playing that role. Friends was all they *should* be. Plan B was just fine. But when it came time to end their dalliance — yeah, that would be a harsh period. She would not get over Caris quickly, but she would prefer to be with Caris for this little time than never at all.

Remember the pros of not being with Caris for a long time. The baby, for one.

Lena heard the *skkkk-skkkk-skkkk* rattle of Shirley's snores when they were halfway up the stairs. "That's awful."

They tiptoed into Shirley's room. Caris got the baby monitor and nudged Shirley awake. "I'm home."

The nursery was painted light green. A wooden crib was in the corner, but a bassinet was the middle of the room. A diaper changing table and Winnie the Pooh decorations rounded the nursery out.

Caris went to the bassinet.

Please look after your little brother or sister after I'm gone. Please tell him or her I was a good person.

Lena surveyed the space, guilt knotting her stomach. She had avoided Donovan. Why? To punish her mother? Or because she hadn't felt comfortable with her stepmother? Both? Because she was afraid Donovan would remind her of two other babies?

Caris lifted the baby, held his face to hers, kissed him, and whispered soothingly: "Mama's home." He was clad only in a diaper, and she patted his bottom. "Dry. For now. Hey, Donovan. Do you remember your sister? She looks scary, but if you ignore the fangs, she's pretty nice."

Lena forced a smile and prodded herself closer to the baby. She hadn't come to spend time with Donovan. Nope. She'd come to spend time with his mother.

Caris continued: "I'm not very happy with your sister right now. She cut my ass off and hung it up to dry at the bowling alley. You want her to teach you how to bowl? Yeah? So you can beat your poor mama too?"

"You're obsessed with me beating you, aren't you?"

"Two hundred and eleven!" Caris shook her head in amazement. "I want your autograph."

A moment later, Caris lowered herself and the baby in a rocking chair. "This will take about twenty minutes."

"All right."

"Oh, hey, do you want to do it?"

"Some other time." *Like never.* Lena sat on the floor and rested her back against the wall. Caris used a pillow on her lap for support. She wrapped her arm around Donovan's upper body and held his head in the crook of her arm. He sucked greedily. After a few minutes, Caris placed a cloth on her shoulder and burped him. "He needs to be burped every three ounces or so," Caris explained. A few minutes later, she asked: "Why don't you want kids? Or do you want them and say you don't?"

"Why screw a kid up? I'd rather use my time for other things." Lena wanted to add a "but." *But I wouldn't mind getting to know your son. Not because he's my brother, but because you're his mother.* Lena turned the question back on Caris. "Why do you want kids?"

"You know, I'm not sure. I didn't want to get pregnant this early. If at all. I was doing so well at work, but Dale...Did your mom tell you? We were going to adopt an older child someday."

"She didn't tell me."

Caris sighed. "Then she came home with a baby book and a story about seeing a cute kid at a park and how you used to be magic in her life, and she wanted a baby, and..." Caris burped Donovan. "I didn't mind. I was excited about the baby. I never thought about not having kids. One of these things that just is."

"It's an open adoption. What I did."

Caris nodded. "I figured."

"Mom wanted me to, to, uh...to keep them."

Caris's brow flickered. "I see."

"She said I'd regret giving them away. She said they were family and that she'd help me. She'd hire a nanny or something. No sense giving them away since she had money and I could still have my own life, a teenager's life. I don't think she forgave me for giving them away. She drove me to see them for visitations and came in with me, but she never played with them. She hasn't asked about them in years."

"I'm sorry."

Lena shrugged. "Them's the breaks. I'll show you their pictures when we're done here."

Caris grinned. "I'll hurry up, then. Hey, do you know any nursery rhymes?"

Lena searched her brain and came up with fragments and snatches. *Strikkke!* "No. A line here and there." She resolved to learn at least two nursery rhymes. She would impress Caris.

Caris hummed, light and melodic: "Twinkle, twinkle, little star, how I wonder what you are. Up above the world so high, like a diamond in the sky. Twinkle, twinkle, little star, How I wonder what you are!"

Donovan's only sounds were gurgles, and Caris smiled and continued: "When the blazing sun is gone, when there's nothing he shines upon, then you show your little light. Twinkle, twinkle, through the night. Twinkle, twinkle, little star, how I wonder what you are!"

Lena got up. She felt like a mouse among cats. This was her mother's wife and child. This magic was meant for Dale, not Lena. "Can I wait for you in your bedroom? Or somewhere?"

Caris betrayed no reaction. "Sure."

"I just—I—I feel weird. Mom should be here. Not me."

Caris rose from the chair. "Let's come up with a rhyme together."

They sat against the wall, and Lena wondered if Caris was conscious of their legs brushing each other. The electricity of their legs. Lena wanted to jump her and—*shh. Stop.*

"I'll start." Caris thought a few seconds. "Twinkle, twinkle, cows gone wild."

Lena giggled. "Cows gone wild? As in girls gone wild?"

Caris's gaze held a devilish gleam. She held the baby up and brought his nose to hers. She sang: "Twinkle, twinkle, cows gone wild, flashing their boobies, oh what's that, looks like a duck, nope, a plane, nope, oh, it's the cows gone wild with their big boobies!"

Donovan grinned widely.

Lena's heart turned over, and her stomach prickled. God. No resisting Caris. She had never wanted to kiss Caris more.

Caris shot Lena a sidelong glance. "Want to try a rhyme?"

"Sure." Lena found herself taking the baby. She held him against her left arm, and he cooed. He was actually kinda cute. Smelled good, like powder.

"He looks like you," Lena said.

"You think?"

"He has your horns and the—" Lena circled his nose. "See here. The hairy mole."

"My mole's uglier."

"Well, yes. And hairier. I was trying to be nice." Lena brought Donovan's face to hers and kissed his forehead. His cheeks. "I eat babies," Lena said. "Hear that, baby? I am gonna eat you. Probably with lettuce and tomatoes. Glug glug glug!" She pretended to chew him. "Gonna eat you like this." Another pretend-chew kiss.

The crying started low, like a keening—a gasp, gasp, wheeze, gasp but then Donovan must have reached back into his lungs because he roared like a hurricane. His wails pierced Lena's eardrums and snaked down to her toes, but Caris's expression was one of faint amusement. "Well, how about that."

"Guess he doesn't want me to eat him?"

Caris took her son. "Shh, baby. Shh." She rose and paced the room. "Shh. Shh."

A moment later, Shirley entered the room. She wore a limp pink sleeping gown. She took the baby from Caris in an automatic gesture.

The crying gradually downgraded to a sniffling.

"Did you two have fun bowling?" Shirley asked.

"Yep," Lena said. *Ew.* She wrinkled her nose. "What's that smell?"

Shirley frowned. "Now, Donovan. Did you make a stinky? Yes, yes, you did!" She cocked an eyebrow at Caris and held the baby out. "He's yours."

*****

In Caris's bedroom, Caris tugged her shoes off. She flopped onto the bed. "Ugh." She poked an eye open. Started laughing. Before long, Lena was laughing too.

After their laughter subsided, Lena wandered to the closet. She found Dale's favorite shirt, a blue polo. She held the garment to her nose. The cologne scent was bracing. "The smell is strong enough to last a year," Lena said. "Drove me crazy. Mom's worse than a skunk. How did you stand it?"

"Don't know," Caris mumbled.

Lena hung the shirt back up and sat on the bed. "Tell me how you met my mother."

"You know how we met."

"Yeah, I know that you interviewed her and the rest was history. I'd like to know more. The details. Your first date, all that." A pause. "If that's okay."

Caris nodded reluctantly. "I was an assistant manager at Stacko. It's like Staples."

"I know where it is."

"We were having problems with the IRS. Audits, what fun. We needed a very specialized attorney. So, the manager, accountant and I interviewed a few people. Your mother was last. She was trying too hard to impress Mr. Fellows. The manager. Her voice was too earnest. She laughed a little too loud at his jokes. Mr. Fellows had to take a phone call at one point. I leaned over and whispered to your mother: 'You're trying too hard.' Dale straightened and patted her hair defensively. She didn't take my advice when Mr. Fellows returned.

"In the end, Mr. Fellows told Dale he'd decided to go elsewhere. On your mother's way out, she reached for my arm. 'Ma'am,' she said. 'You were right. I apologize. I'd like to take you to dinner tomorrow night and pick your brain.' "

"Mmm. Kinda sweet, actually."

"Speaking of work, I have to do my milking job now. Will you wait a few minutes?"

"No problem." *I want to watch…*

*****

When Caris returned, Lena was on the bed, asleep, her ponytail spread below her. Caris studied the swell of her breasts, the curve of her butt, the length of her thighs, and Caris's chest ached.

Lena flickered an eye open. "How'd the milking go?"

"My udders held up. They're improving. Lena?"

"Hmm?"

"Can I lay with you? For a few minutes?"

"It's your bed." Lena scooted over, and Caris noticed Lena was careful to keep a distance from her.

"I wish you could stay with me tonight," Caris whispered.

Lena looked away.

"I didn't mean like that," Caris said quickly. "I meant that—Never mind."

"I know what you meant."

"Good, because I'm not sure what I meant." Caris realized that their legs and ankles were touching. Just a bit. Yes, this was nice. Exactly what Caris needed.

Lena glanced at the nightstand clock. Midnight. "I hate to do this, but I have to get to bed. Early morning."

Caris's heart crashed. *Parole is over. Back to prison.* "You said you'd show me their pictures."

Lena sighed. "Yep." She got her cellphone out. "The Soundros family. Mommy, daddy, their children."

A handsome family greeted Caris. The mother and father were black, although the mother had almond-shaped eyes. Asian blood, maybe. The children, *Lena's children*—Caris lost herself in them. Their smiles were identical, tilted to the right side. The boy looked a lot like Lena, despite his dark skin. Looked a hell of a lot like Lena, actually. Same eyes, nose, chin.

"Aron looks like Deonte," Lena said.

"She's beautiful. They both are. Like you." Caris reluctantly gave the phone back.

"You think Mom was right? Should I have kept them?"

Caris was not sure what to say. One thing she knew: Lena did not need more grief or self-doubt. "I think your mother was wrong not to fully support your decision. She should have played with the children and... I would have. I would now."

Lena could not meet her eyes. "I better go."

"Right. Well, I'll walk you out. The living room is dangerous in the dark."

George had left the lamp on, but Caris went outside anyway. The night was refreshing and nippy. A little wind. Caris would stay outside for a while after Lena left. And think about Lena. Then go inside and rub the memories of Lena's touches into her pussy.

Caris and Lena strolled the few feet to her car. "Good night," Caris said. She glanced at the sky. Nice night. Lots of stars out, practically a different sky from the smudgy one right after bowling. *That's right. Think about stars and not about how much you want to kiss Lena.*

"Good night." Lena smiled. Made no move to get into her car. Caris made no move to turn around.

"I need to be absolutely clear with you," Caris said. "In case it was not clear earlier. I don't want a relationship. Don't need a relationship. I have so much going on. I'm right out of a marriage." Caris did not quite believe what she said. For one thing, Dale had begun freezing her out long before Donovan was born. Dale and Caris had been distancing themselves emotionally from each other. And Caris had a feeling she and Lena could be happy together. Very. But easier to be cooler and distant at this point. Meet Lena on her terms.

Lena blinked. An astonished blink, as if to say how could anyone in her right mind infer that she and Caris were headed for a relationship? "I don't want a relationship either," Lena said. "With anyone." She laughed. "Can you imagine us in a relationship? Grandma and Granddad would have heart attacks."

"Right," Caris said, thinking Lena had not needed to be quite so fervent in her agreement. "So that's out of the way. Can I kiss you now?"

Lena's answer was to draw Caris into her arms. The first kiss was on the mouth, like a whisper, like the two half-second nothing kisses the night before, and a whisper that caused Caris's toes to curl. Then came a hard, desperate kiss, and more toe curls. Lena tasted of beer, the same beer Caris had, and Lena's mouth was soft, her tongue eager and the right degree of wet. Their kiss was like a conversation, allowing Caris to express to Lena what she could not verbalize, and Lena was an excellent conversationalist.

Chapter 14

Caris showered, dressed and grabbed a banana. The weather was nice on a Saturday, Dale's fifth day at Pinewood, and Caris figured she would take Donovan to see his other mother for a while. Dale was in bed, her eyes closed. "She had a good night," one of the nurses said. "No problems. She's adjusting nicely."

Shirley was not around. Not yet, anyway. *Good.* Shirley and George had moved out the day before, and last night without them had been nice. Liberating. Caris had stripped naked and stayed that way all night, even as she watched TV on the couch. Plus, Shirley's hovering got on Caris's nerves.

Pinewood was peaceful. Quieter. None of the urgency that permeated the hospital. Caris pulled the curtains back from Dale's windows and tugged up the blinds to let the sun shine through. "It's a beautiful morning," she told Dale. "Feels like fall's coming early."

Dale was awake. *Blink. Blink.*

Caris summoned Joe, her favorite orderly. Joe was gentle and had muscles the size of the Grand Canyon. He made transferring Dale to the wheelchair look easy. "Here we go, Mrs. Ismay," he said brightly to Dale. He slid his arms under her and lifted. "Nice and easy."

She would hate this. Dale, fiercely independent and prideful, would die before subjecting herself to this. *Stop it. She does deserve her second chance.* Pitiful now did not mean pitiful later. Plenty of room to go back up.

Caris carried Donovan outside, and Joe wheeled Dale. Caris inhaled the welcome scent of freshly mowed grass. Birds chirped. Perfect Disney setting, indeed. She chose a spot at the banks of the duck pond. A few ducks, some with babies, paddled in the water.

"You can feed them bread and rice cakes," Joe said.

"Cool. Thanks."

"See you soon."

Caris unfurled a checkered picnic blanket. *Lena, Lena, Lena. What are you doing to me?*

Donovan tried to haul himself across the blanket, toward an approaching duck. "Ba! La! Ba ba!"

Caris was ready to leave already. "Hey, Mr. Ba La. Let's get Mama a dress."

*****

Caris and Donovan headed to Space. Caris pondered the black dress again. She wouldn't fit in the size eight, but she could try a size ten.

The dress hugged her curves. It was simple, understated. Versatile. Equally great for dinner and a movie or for a black-tie event, with the proper accessories. Maybe dinner tomorrow with Lena? Caris imagined Lena's eyes going wide and later, Lena peeling the dress off.

No. Caris should save this dress for a date. A true date. Jennifer said she had a few people in mind for Caris and had suggested a double date.

Caris studied her breasts. They were definitely bouncing back. On her stomach, some stretch marks were gone, others lighter.

An image of Lena teasing her nipple popped up. Lena rubbing the nipple, pinching it, nibbling it between her white teeth. Caris's nipples hardened. Her clit hardened.

Caris continued studying herself in the mirror, awe spreading through her body. *I'm a woman again.*

And she wanted Lena.

Caris dialed Jennifer. "Let's try your double date idea. And do you mind watching Donovan for a few hours tonight?"

After Caris hung up, Donovan waved his fists in the air and shot her a grin. She smiled back. Before long, the belly swollen with her son and the milk weighing down her breasts would be dim memories. Maybe she'd laugh about her cow tits one day, when she was eighty-two. Shirley's age. *What I'd give to be young and to have these milky breasts back, to have my child be a baby again and nearby instead of ignoring my phone calls or in a persistent vegetative state.*

She recalled Lena, younger than her, and regretting letting her children go. Caris imagined being forced to give up Donovan. No way.

An intense love overwhelmed Caris. The thought of losing Donovan was unbearable. The thought of losing Lena was unbearable.

Caris took her son in her arms and cradled him. "I love you, baby," she said. "Mama loves you."

*****

That night, Lena's bug was parked behind Azizi, and Caris's heart leapt.

But no.

She needed to stay the hell away from Lena.

Twenty minutes later, Caris took a left shortly before the Ben Brenman park off Route 236. She pulled into the Almond's parking lot. Mostly full. Looked like it held about fifteen spaces. Good lighting. Almond's was a squat, square orange-ish building. Not what Caris had expected. She could not find the name anywhere.

So, this was it. Where Dale last lived. Spoke her last words. Slipped a note into Lena's tote bag and bid sayonara, au revior, seeyalater.

Caris sat at the bar, near a male bartender and a college-aged couple. The bartender was obscured in the shadows. He watched the Braves on TV, his back to Caris and the couple. The man in the couple was a Mr. Abercrombie and Fitch. The woman was a young, plump Betty Crocker, red shirt and all.

"You all right?" the bartender asked.

Caris ordered a margarita. "Lovely." She kept her eyes fastened on the couple, hoping the bartender would get the message and leave her alone.

Poor Betty Crocker. Betty hung onto Mr. Abercrombie's every word, leaned into him, adored him with dumb brown doe eyes. Mr. Abercrombie grunted in response and poked texts into his cellphone. Betty would not give up. She purred into his ear, her hands disappearing below the bar counter.

Caris licked her margarita salt.

Mr. Abercrombie put his cellphone away. Ordered another beer. "Shit, Betty. Stop pawing. A few more minutes, okay. Then we'll go to your place."

Caris lifted her glass, concealing her grin. *Damn. Her name IS Betty.*

"They come every once in a while," the bartender remarked. "She's hopeless, isn't she? He uses her, and she doesn't have the self-respect to stand up for herself."

Caris did not bother to reply. Sometimes respect was underrated. Of course they were going to Betty's place. Mr. Abercrombie probably had roommates. Roommates he did not want to know about Betty, who was desperate and whom he probably considered several levels below him in the looks department.

Was it time to bring out Melanie Michaels after — how long had it been — five or so years? In her younger days, Caris would go out sometimes to bars or clubs and pick up women. She would give her name as Melanie Michaels, her porn star name. First pet: Melanie, the doomed little mouse. Street she grew up on: Michaels Avenue.

But this was a straight bar. In suburbia. *Try it. Odder things have happened.* It would get her mind, her body, off Lena.

Caris flashed her smile for practice. She could not see it, of course, but the smile was more of a confidence thing, more like a feeling. No mirror required. Caris nailed the smile on her second attempt. She still had that elusive *it*, that joie de vivre. When her eyes twinkled that mischievous twinkle, Betty would be a goner.

Ten minutes later, Mr. Abercrombie said: "Gotta drain the lizard and make another call." He walked off, big important man swaggering, jewels to protect between his legs.

Betty followed him, but disappeared into the women's bathroom. Perfect.

Caris waited until Betty washed her hands. "Your boyfriend is jerking you around."

Betty narrowed her eyes. "He's a nice guy."

Caris leaned into her. She made sure her breath tickled Betty's ear. "He doesn't go down on you. Doesn't give you screaming orgasms. I will." *But you won't touch me. Anywhere. Wham bam, thank you, ma'am.*

Betty stepped back. Her doe eyes were wide, captured in car headlights. Caris let her take a moment to process the turn of events.

Curiosity and a half smile, a let's see now played across Betty's face. "Who are you? Did Todd send you?"

"I'm Melanie Michaels. Or whoever you want me to be." Caris moved her mouth over Betty's, devouring its softness. She tasted cheap rum on Betty's tongue and felt an intense pain, an intense ache for Lena's mouth. Lena's tongue. Betty gasped and moaned.

"Your place?" Caris asked. "Or here?"

Betty's eyes were luminous, her cheeks flushed, but she said: "Um, that was amazing, but I better go."

*****

After Caris got home and bade Jennifer goodbye, she slid into the bathtub. She shaved her armpits and her legs. She trimmed her pussy and shaved the edges of her pussy and her lips, creating easy, smooth access. She and Lena fit, no denying it. They just did. Hard to explain. Caris had been in a dark place since before Dale's accident, and now there was a light. The light was not where Caris had expected it to be. Was not where she wanted it to be. But there was a light.

Anyway, was it such a big deal whom she would be doing things with? *Yes. Of course it is.*

Says who? Show me the rule book.

After the shave and trim, Caris worked even more deliberately. She rubbed waterproof lube on her clit. She teased herself until she could wait no longer. Her orgasm was tremendous but only whetted her desire for Lena.

Caris was back at Pinewood the next day. She had not planned on returning so soon, but Shirley had called and asked her to come about noon.

When Caris and Donovan arrived, only Dale was in the room. Caris picked up an Agatha Christie book on Dale's nightstand. It was a collection of three short stories: *Crooked House, Ordeal by Innocence* and *The Seven Dials Mystery.* Shirley needed a new copy. The book was worn, dog-eared. Caris studied it carefully. The alternative was to study Dale carefully.

Caris sat and cleared her throat. "Crooked House," she began. "Chapter One. I first came to know Sophia Leonides in Egypt towards the end of the war. She held a fairly high administrative post...You know what, Dale? I bet you're sick of Agatha Christie. I don't know how your mom does all that reading, all the time." Caris snapped the book shut and reached for the newspaper at the foot of the bed. She scanned the sports section. "No Braves news. Sorry." The Braves were Dale's favorite baseball team.

Nothing.

"Yeah. It's not exactly overwhelming, is it? Okay, then. Back to Sophia Leonides." Caris scanned a couple of paragraphs. "She's a fox. Seems she's extremely easy to look at. She has a clear mind and a dry sense of humor. She's easy to talk to and enjoys dancing."

Blank stare.

"Caris." Lena's voice.

Caris snapped her head up. Lena was hovering in the doorway.

"Hi," Lena said with a smile.

"Hi, Lena. It's good to see you." Polite, everyday dialogue. As if they hadn't experienced perfect kisses, that conversation of a kiss.

"I can come back in a few minutes if—"

"No. Stay. Did your grandmother summon you here, too?"

Lena stepped into the room. "Yep. So, tell me more about Sophia Leonides."

Caris scanned a few lines in the book. "Sophia has dark, crisp hair. A fighting chin. She is a good listener but doesn't like to talk about herself. She likes how this guy, Charles, has a funny way of doing things."

"Sophia reminds me of you."

"How?"

Lena winked. "She's a fox."

Caris could not help but smile.

"So who is this Charles?"

Caris surveyed the next couple of pages. Nothing much. "I don't know." She closed the book, giving Lena a playful gaze. "Who do you think he is?"

"Hmm." Lena puckered her lips. "He's a double agent. His funny way of doing things is a cover. In actuality, he's a ruthless assassin."

"His assignment is to kill Sophia."

"Sophia, whom he doesn't know is his sister."

Caris leaned forward, caught up in the game. "Sophia is also nosy. One day, she's ruffling through Charles's luggage and finds an old family photo. It falls into place. She realizes who he is. She has to decide between her duty to her country or to her illegitimate brother. She has no idea he wants to kill her. Furthermore — "

A cry. A stomp. Shirley brushing past Lena. "That's not how it happens," she huffed. "Not even close. Move over!" She flapped her arm, motioning Caris aside.

"Grandma, we were only having fun," Lena protested. "You can play, too."

Shirley grabbed the book. "That's not how it happens! This isn't play. Let's not confuse Dale."

Be that way. No new copy for you.

"Why are we here, Grandma?"

Shirley's expression turned cool and distant. "Your grandfather is at the condo packing. He and I have been having problems. He's moving back to Rhode Island next week."

Lena shifted her weight. "Wow. Sorry."

Caris squeezed Shirley's shoulder. She was sure that under Shirley's icy veneer was a world of pain and hurt. She had to admit, though, that the news did not surprise her. She did not blame George for leaving. Shirley was obsessed with Dale. Spent her time with Dale and most of her conversations were about Dale — researching treatments, the leaps and bounds science was bound to make, how they ought to pray, et cetera. George had become furniture to Shirley. She discounted his opinions and did not listen to him.

"I'm sorry, Shirley. Anything I can do?"

"I'm fine," Shirley said. "Just as well. Dale needs all of my focus. *Our* focus. George thinks — " She scoffed. "He thinks Dale's dead. He thinks our baby's dead. He's thought so all along." She shot Lena a provocative scowl, daring Lena to contradict her.

Lena said nothing.

Caris said nothing.

Donovan slept.

Caris tried to see Dale through fresh, unbiased eyes. Gray hair. Sunken chest, weak. Non-expressive. Dale's gown was more alive than

Dale was. Dale was an it. Not a he or she. *That isn't a person. That's a zombie corpse.* What was in the bed was a husk. Dale's once-strong chest was paper-thin. Her jowls sagged. She had lost forty pounds. Her muscle tone was going. The nursing home staff played music for Dale, flexed her arms and legs, but there was only so much they could do.

The opposite had been happening for Shirley. As her daughter withered, Shirley grew.

Shirley reached into the nightstand drawer and drew out a tattered book. "Let's finish *Ten Little Indians.*"

Lena sighed, a helpless sigh. She pulled her ponytail loose, sat on the floor and rested her head, uptilted, against the wall. She closed her eyes.

Caris sat at a round corner table. She cradled Donovan and, soothed by the rise and fall of Shirley's voice, watched Lena, Shirley and Dale. Mostly Lena. Her long eyelashes. The dark loose hair almost halfway down her back.

Caris's whole body hurt. Lena infiltrated her thoughts, her waking moments. Caris could count on two fingers the number of people she had been in love with.

Alexandra, her first girlfriend.

Dale.

Lena could join that list very, very easily. With the slightest nudge. Maybe already had.

Caris's love for Alexandra had developed over time, in high school. Caris's love for Dale had developed slowly, too. Caris almost had not accepted Dale's request for a second date, but something whispered in her ear to, so she had. A few months later, she was firmly in love.

Now this thing with Lena. This thing that wasn't a thing. Did she want to be in love with Lena, especially at this time in her life? No, of course not.

But there it was, and it was different from what she had felt for Alexandra and Dale. Caris could not explain it. On a higher plane, somehow. Perhaps because of their circumstances. No denying they were going through a highly emotional experience together. Essential to remember: *You are not in love with Lena. The situation makes you think you are.*

Lena opened her eyes. She met Caris's gaze and smiled, a little sad, secret smile. Caris's skin prickled, and she felt Lena's tongue again playing hide and seek with hers. Caris imagined Lena's hands rubbing her back, and then her breasts. They might as well be in bed, their arms and legs entwined, so intimate and poignant was Lena's smile.

"One little Indian boy left all alone," Shirley read. "He went out and hanged himself, and then there were none."

Chapter 15

Caris, Lena and Donovan left together. "I have a date this Saturday," Caris said. "Sort of. It's a double date with Jennifer, Oliver and a friend of theirs. Her name's Patricia White. Probably gonna amount to nothing, but..."

Lena smiled, but it did not reach her eyes. "That's good. I could baby-sit Donovan while you're on your date."

"No."

"Why?"

"Not while I'm on a date, Lena."

Lena's responding grin was casual. "What's the big deal? Babysitting is babysitting."

Did Lena really think that? Or was she protecting herself? Didn't matter. The answer was no either way. Caris shook her head. "Not while I'm on a date. That's too tacky."

Lena jammed her hands in her pockets. "Fine. Whatever. Look, I have to be at work soon, but do you have a minute to stop by my place? I want your opinion on something."

*****

In the apartment, Lena zipped her backpack open, hoping she was not about to make a colossal mistake. Donovan was sleeping, and Caris had kept him in his baby carrier seat or whatever it was called, and set him on the floor.

Lena got three books from her backpack. She laid them, covers up, on the kitchen table. Books on taking care of infants and toddlers.

Caris blinked. Several more blinks. Confused blinks.

Lena felt the walls close in on her. *What are you doing, Lena Alice Ismay?* "I'm sorry I haven't been around to help with Donovan, but I want to be. It's what Mom would have wanted. Ah, screw that. It's what I want. For several reasons. Uh..." Lena rubbed her forehead. She pretended to be engrossed in the cover of one book: a baby in pink.

"I don't have much family left," she went on. "Grandma and Grandpa are old. Healthy, but old. After they're gone, it's going to be just me unless I..." Lena sighed. "I've realized that...eh. Never mind. Thing is, I have you.

I have Donovan. Why aren't I taking advantage of that? Mom's going to die, she won't be here this time next year, and you'll meet someone eventually. Marry someone else. That woman will be Donovan's other mother. Mom isn't his mother. She gave up that right, but I don't want to make the same mistake Mom did. I know Grandma and Granddad love him as much as they love me. Doesn't matter he's not their biological grandchild and that Mom was never his mother. When you get married again, he'll still be their grandchild. I want him to be my brother, too. No matter what." *You're babbling.* Lena forced herself to slow down.

"I'm rambling nonsense, but what I'm trying to say is that if there's an emergency or something, I should know how to take care of him. Or even if there isn't an emergency. If you need me to baby-sit, I'll try. I want to do right by him. Anyway, I got these books from the library. Are they any good?"

Caris had tears in her eyes.

Lena touched Caris's arm. "Please don't cry. Because then I'll cry and I really, I—" She grimaced.

Caris wiped at her eyes, preventing her tears from falling. She riffled through the books and said a simple: "They look good. I can lend you a few of mine."

"Good," Lena said briskly. She re-packed the books. "Okay, then. I better get ready for work."

"Something I need to clarify," Caris said slowly. "She *was* Donovan's mother. While I was pregnant. She read to my stomach, and even after she started freezing me out, she went to the doctor appointments. She took charge of getting the nursery together. She was his mother. She was."

"All right," Lena said, aware her voice was a monotone.

"I wanted to clarify. That's all."

"Clarified."

Caris brushed her thumb against Lena's cheek and brought her lips to Lena's. "Let's shut up about her. Can you lay down for a minute before work?"

*****

Lena and Caris lay entwined. Who was holding and comforting whom was unclear, but Caris knew where to rub Lena's back, when to squeeze her. It had been too long since someone strong held Lena. Really held her, like a woman ought to be held. Caroline had tried, sure, but it never had felt quite right. This did. Lena lost herself in Caris's smell, her touch, her closeness, her femaleness.

Lena did not stop Caris when Caris unbuttoned Lena's jeans. In fact, Lena pulled her jeans down partway, and Caris's hand found its way into Lena's underwear.

"You're wet," Caris whispered.

"Fuck me. Please."

So Caris did, and like Lena's earlier orgasm with Caris, this one was quick. No foreplay. Which was how it should be, because they were on Plan B.

Afterward, Lena used the same method on Caris — Caris who was incredibly wet, Caris who clamped her arms around Lena and moaned and moaned. Her orgasm was fast, too, a great shudder.

After they were finished, Caris's breathing gradually became deep, slow and rhythmic, but Lena remained wide awake. She tightened her hold on Caris. This wasn't enough. Stupid, furtive orgasms, no kissing in bed. Dissatisfaction.

"Can we do naked sometime?" Caris murmured.

"I thought you were asleep."

"No."

"Sure, we can do naked sometime. But now I really need to get ready for work."

"This was good, Lena. Thank you."

Lena kissed her on the cheek, a peck. "No problemo. Have a good rest of the day. Call after your date if you want. Hope it goes well."

*****

Lena checked herself over in the mirror Saturday morning. Jeans, green polo shirt. Green so her eyes would be green. She wore new red tennis shoes. The kids would like that, red shoes. Joanna had called Wednesday to say Lena could take the children to the park down their street for two hours Saturday. Just her and the children. Lena surveyed the bag at her side. Just her, the children — and baseball gloves, baseballs, tennis racquets, tennis balls and a few Frisbees. In case no one had anything to say.

Joanna had not said much on the phone. She did not need to. Her tones had been disapproving for three years. No doubt she was afraid that once the children turned eighteen, they would abandon her and gravitate toward Lena. Lena, who had given them up, Lena who did not deserve them.

Lena resolved to tell Joanna that she need not worry about the children picking Lena over her. Joanna did not see how the children looked at her. Joanna was their mother.

At three o'clock, Lena rang the Soundroses' doorbell. She was supposed to be working until eight today, but she had switched shifts. She did not know when she might get another opportunity like this.

Malik answered the door. "Hey, Lena. How ya doing?"

"Good. Fine. Thank you."

Malik smiled. "Great. Good. Well, uh, Nakeem decided he doesn't want to go."

Lena managed to keep her smile up. "Okay," she said. Nakeem was the sensitive one. He had not really made an effort to get to know her when she resurfaced in his life. She did not blame him. She could promise repeatedly she would not lose contact with him again, but why should he believe her? Perhaps he just did not care. He had his mother. He had his father. He had his buddy Deonte. What use did he have for a white woman called Lena?

"So," Malik said, "Nakeem and Joanna are at a movie. Hope you don't mind if I go with you and Aron. I'll..." He lowered his gaze for a second. "Let you guys have some alone time."

"I'd love to have you come. Sure."

"Great." He called for Aron, and she bounced out a moment later.

"Hey, Lena. We got a dog! Her name's Mr. Goodbar. But she's a girl dog. She's a chocolate lab. Nakeem wanted to name her Hershey, but that's kind of obvious, don't you think? So I said: 'Let's call her Mr. Goodbar.' And Nakeem said: 'But she's a girl.' Mom said to call her Ms. Goodbar. Can she come with us? Please?"

"Ask your father."

Malik ruffled Aron's hair. "Go get Ms. Goodbar."

*****

They set off walking down the sidewalk to the park. Aron was in the middle, holding Ms. Goodbar's leash. Aron was a chatterer, always had been. Her topic of conversation today was Ms. Goodbar, who was her first dog.

Lena wished she could look at Aron. No, not look at her. Study her. Examine her. Take her in. Like she could with pictures. Touch her, feel her. Experience the texture of her kinky black hair, of her smooth cheeks. Watch her sleep.

At the park, Ms. Goodbar pooed, and Aron wrinkled her nose and looked up at her father. "Do I have to clean it?"

Malik laughed. "Yep."

They bought Cokes from a machine, and Malik said he would take Ms. Goodbar for a stroll around the park.

Lena's mind was a blank as Malik and the puppy left. She was about to reach into her pocket for a list of questions she had prepared for this exact occurrence when Aron piped up: "Nakeem doesn't like you. He says Deonte's better than you."

"Oh."

"I like you, though."

"I like you, too. And Nakeem."

Aron fiddled with the tab on her Coke can. *Crackle crackle crackle.* "Can I stay with you sometime?" she mumbled.

"That's up to your parents."

"Nakeem's stupid."

"No, sweetie. He's not."

"Is too."

Lena winked at the child. "I don't make stupid kids."

Aron's lips tugged into a little smile. *Crackle crackle.* "Your mom was in a wreck."

Lena licked suddenly dry lips. "Yes."

"I Google your name a lot. And her name, too."

"Sure, why not."

"Is your mom okay?"

"She's in a persistent vegetative state. Do you know what that is? It's like a coma. She probably won't come out of it." Lena scanned the park for Malik; he was halfway around.

Aron studied her Coke can thoughtfully. "I didn't tell Nakeem or Mom and Dad about the wreck."

"That's fine. You don't have to tell them everything."

"I wouldn't mind going to see your mom." *Crackle.* "If you wanted. I'd be cool with it."

"She doesn't look good."

"What's she look like?"

"Not like a person. Like she has no feeling. No awareness."

"How come you don't hug me? Or touch me?"

"I hug you," Lena protested. "I hugged you after dinner at Applebee's."

"Oh." Aron bit her lip. "Guess so. Do you have a boyfriend?"

Lena sipped from her Coke. She had never told Malik and Joanna she was gay. If they had a problem with it, Lena did not want them using the gay issue to keep the children from her. "No," Lena said. "No boyfriend. Work and school keep me really busy."

"You jealous about Deonte gettin' married?"

"I'm happy for him."

"You wanna be with him?"

Lena grinned. "No. Hey, you going to the wedding? I think I might."

Aron glowered. "I can't. Mom says we're on vacation. But she didn't tell me about the vacation until I asked."

"I'm sorry."

"Is your mom nice?"

"Mmm, she's—yeah. She's nice. I have a stepmother. She's very nice."

"You mean stepfather?"

"My mother is married to a woman."

Aron's eyes lit up. "Oh! Like your mom's gay. Cool. I got a gay uncle."

Lena allowed herself a relieved breath. "That's great, Aron. I showed my stepmother your picture. She said you're beautiful."

"I guess you're kind of like my stepmother, aren't you, Lena?"

"That's one way to look at it."

"Hey, girls." Malik was back.

"Hi, Daddy."

Lena got out the Frisbee, and the three of them played for about an hour. Then it was time to head back. Malik put his arm around Aron's shoulder, she held Ms. Goodbar's leash in one hand, and after a moment, used her free hand to take Lena's hand.

Aron's hand was small. Callused. Perfect. Lena never wanted to let go. She hoped Joanna would let her daughter stay with Lena one night. *Please, please.* She would love to eat popcorn with Aron, watch movies with her, and maybe they could do each other's hair.

At the house, she hugged Aron—a good hug—marveled at how thin and bony the girl was, and kissed Aron on the cheek. "Bye, sweetie."

"Bye, Lena." Aron kissed her back. "I hope your mom gets better."

*****

Caris decided that night not to wear the black dress. She would save it for Lena. She riffled through the closet and settled on a pair of black pants and a dressy blue shirt.

Patricia White seemed nice. She was good-looking. Athletic. Butch. Somewhat like a younger version of Dale, if Dale had a tan, spiky blond hair and blue eyes. Patricia did not ask about Dale. Jennifer had debriefed her on the situation, and Patricia probably knew this outing was casual, very casual. She should not be expecting anything serious from it.

They ate at Mr. Chen's, a new Chinese restaurant. Patricia had a child too, a nine-year-old boy, and they talked about him. Jennifer and Oliver discussed having kids, maybe in the next couple of years. After dinner, the four of them went to the symphony.

Nice night. Nice conversation. Nowhere near nice enough to get Caris's mind off Lena.

*****

Caris's call came just after midnight. Lena was on her bed in the dark and secretly hoping the date had crashed and burned. Been from hell.

"How did it go?" Lena asked. She imagined Caris's lips covering hers hungrily. Caris mounting her. Imagined Caris mounting her faceless date.

"She was cute. Nice."

"Going out with her again?"

"I might."

Lena made a fist around her bed sheets. "Great. Happy for you. What'd you all do?"

"We went to dinner, then the symphony."

"Awesome."

"One big problem with her. Makes me have second thoughts about going out with her again."

"Yeah?"

"She has a tail that leaves orange goo everywhere she walks."

Lena grinned and closed her eyes. *Be still, my heart.* "Does she clean up after herself?"

"She has a robot dog who licks the goo." Caris paused. "You okay?"

"I'm good."

"I don't want to hurt you," Caris whispered.

"You're not. One of the best things for you right now is to go out and meet people. I'm fine." Lena squeezed the bed sheets again. "I have my life. I'm not a jealous person." And she was not, she really was not. "I've had a few nonexclusive relationships. Not that we're in a relationship. But you know what I meant."

"Are you going out with other people?"

"Work and school keep me busy enough."

"I don't feel right going out with people if you're not."

"Me dating other people is the least of our issues, don't you think?"

"I—okay. You're right."

"Look, Caris. Go out and have fun. Meet people. You don't need to tell me when you have dates. We should probably, uh, I'll go on a few dates, all right? Will that make you happy?"

"Probably for the best," Caris whispered.

"I'm actually really busy the next few weeks." *No, I'm not. I'm my usual ordinary busy.* "So this is a good time for you to go out lots."

"No problem. Um, okay. Well, give me a ring when you're free. We'll do something."

"Caris, wait a sec."

"Yeah?"

"I—I didn't mean—I really am busy."

"Give me a ring when you're free, okay? Take care."

"Wait."

Caris hung up. "Shit!" Lena said. "Shit, shit!" *Don't you dare sabotage this. She's too good for you to do this to her.*

Lena dialed Caris, and Caris answered on the third ring. "Can I come over?" Lena asked. "Give you a good night kiss? Please?"

A hesitation, then a soft: "Okay."

"And can I…" Lena swallowed. "I saw Aron today. It went— it was okay. I'd like to tell you about it. Caris, do you know you're the only person I've told about the children?"

"I am?"

"Yes."

"Why?"

Lena shrugged. "Because I never wanted to tell anyone else. Besides, you needed the distraction."

"I'm glad you told me."

"So am I. I'm very glad."

Chapter 16

The next day, Lena was annoyed. Every time she showed up at Pinewood, Shirley was there.

Every. Damn. Time.

The thought that Lena might want to be alone with her mother for a few minutes apparently did not occur to Shirley. Lena accepted that it was partly her fault. She never hinted. She showed up, kissed Dale, listened to Shirley read a while, then left.

Today, though, Lena had enough. Shirley and a couple of nurses had dressed Dale in regular clothes, and Shirley was about to take Dale to the duck pond.

"Hey, Grandma. You look like you need a break. I'll take Mom outside, and you go out for coffee or something. Bring me back a frappuccino."

Shirley blinked, but understanding dawned in her expression. "Of course, sweetie."

Lena scribbled down her order, and Shirley left. Lena pushed her mother in the wheelchair outside. Lena liked the duck pond, but lots of people were out today. No problem. Pinewood's grounds were expansive. Lena found an isolated bench off a walking trail and applied the wheelchair brake.

"You look good today." Dale wore sweat pants and a blue T-shirt.

"Me? You like my shirt too?" Lena shot her mother a rueful glance. "No, it's not new. Remember, Mom? Every time you see this shirt, you ask if it's new. Anyway, I figure we have maybe thirty minutes. I've been wanting to talk to you. Uh, I met someone."

And it's because of that someone I am pleasantly sore this morning. Caris had finger fucked Lena last night, with three fingers. For a long time. No urgency to it, just a deep, rhythmic in and out, and *God*. Lena had loved it.

Caris had welcomed Lena with a smile. They got into bed — not naked, though. Caris did the finger fucking thing, and Lena talked. Talked while Caris fucked her, yep. She told Caris about Aron and about Nakeem, and about what being pregnant with twins was like. The ache and the pain of the memories had been dull and distant last night, because Lena was with Caris, Caris was inside her, and the world was right.

A robin landed on the walking path. Dale fastened her gaze on the robin, and Lena shivered. Papers and doctors could say what they wanted to say, but it was damn eerie how once in a while, her mother truly seemed to be attentive. To random things, though. That was how Lena knew for sure it meant nothing. If her mother was going to be attentive, wouldn't be to a damn bird.

Shirley loved pointing out when Dale seemed to track objects and people. "Her eyes are following the nurse around the room," Shirley whispered one time. Not in Lena's opinion, but whatever. Once, though, she'd thought her mother was watching trees sway outside the window. The day was windy, and the trees moved like they were watching a tennis match. So did Dale's gaze, for a precious ten or fifteen seconds. *Tricks of the mind.*

The robin stepped on a leaf. *Crackle.*

Blink blink blink.

"Cute bird," Lena murmured.

The robin flew away. Dale's gaze remained transfixed to the spot on the walking path.

"Hey, Mom, so I met someone. Uh...I really like her. I'm thinking about sending her flowers tomorrow. Roses, probably. Kinda boring, and I'm trying to think of something more interesting. Not candy. But, hey. Roses will do, right? Nothing wrong with being old-fashioned and romantic once in a while."

Lena's chest was about to burst. She wanted to say more. So much more. That she was falling in love, truly in love, and quite possibly for the first time in her life. Lena wanted to say the woman's name. That she had a baby. That this new woman was different, that Lena could see many, many years with her. Perhaps a lifetime. The doctors said Dale was dead. Her brain was nothing. But in case Dale flickered in there somewhere, Lena would say nothing identifiable.

Lena glanced around her, feeling foolish for what she was about to perform. She adjusted Dale's wheelchair so Dale faced her. "Blink once for yes. Twice for no." Lena made a thumbs-up. "Am I holding up any fingers?"

No blinks.

Lena frowned. "A thumb isn't a finger. You're right. You and your lawyer mind, huh?" She let herself laugh.

Blink blink blink.

Lena held up her pointer finger. "Am I holding up one finger?"

Blink.

Lena's heart nearly stopped. Coincidence.

"Are we outside?"

Blink blink. Wrong answer.

"We're outside, Mom," Lena said softly. "Let's try another. Is my hair in a ponytail?" The correct answer was *blink.*

Dale went *blink blink blink blink blink.*

"Are your parents Shirley and George?"
Blink blink blink.
"Is my name Lena?"
Blink blink.
Nothing stirred in that brain.
"I miss you, Mom."
Dale grunted, a low, rough sound. *Blink blink blink.*
Lena remembered Caris kissing her, the first time. Caris's three
fingers inside her last night. "I want to make love to her. To tell her I love
her. Is that stupid? Is it too early?"
Dale's eyes were as animated as marbles.
"She says she isn't ready for a relationship, but that's not a problem.
We'll figure out a way. A relationship is what the people in it make it to be.
She can — she deserves to date people. Have her own life. As long as, uh...I
don't know. She loves me back, Mom. I'm pretty sure she does. As long as
she loves me and we communicate openly, we'll be fine. We sure ain't
communicating openly right now. But we're going to talk soon. I'll make
sure of it."
Brown marble eyes. "Time for me to shut up."
Lena wheeled her mother back to the room. No Shirley yet. Lena bent
down and kissed Dale on the forehead. "I love you, Mom. Very much. I'm
sorry I couldn't say it before the wreck."
Dale's eyes drooped shut. Falling asleep.
Shirley returned a few minutes later. "Anything happen?"
"Nothing at all," Lena mumbled.

*****

Caris was worried about her mother-in-law, so the next time Caris
was at Pinewood, she suggested a trip to Shirley. "You, me and Donovan.
Go somewhere to relax and recharge our batteries."
"I can't leave Dale. What if something happens?"
"Nothing will happen. Come on. You know you need a break. I'll take
care of the arrangements."
"I can't leave Dale," Shirley repeated. "Something might happen."
"How about a one-night trip?" Caris had to admit the trip would be
just as much for her as for Shirley. Caris needed a change of scenery. Fresh
air. Something to help get her mind off Lena. Lena and her wet pussy,
Lena with her sighs and little moans. Lena who let Caris fuck her, in and
out for like an hour, Lena who looked at her in that *intense* way.
"I need to be here for Dale," Shirley argued.

Caris looked into Shirley's eyes. Steadfast. Resolute. She was not going anywhere. "Okay," Caris said. "Let me know if you change your mind. Anytime."

*****

Lena was surprised to get a package from Caris two weeks after their night together. They had not talked since. Caris had not called, and Lena had been too scared to contact her, afraid she might tell Caris too much. Come across too strongly: *I love you, Caris, I love you, take your damn clothes off already and let me show you how much I love you...*

The package revealed a black three-ring binder and a note.

Lena:
You might remember in one of my letters, I said I would write down what I remember your mother telling me about your father. I haven't slacked on that. I've been writing stories since that time, and now I think I am finished. Some good stories in there. Some funny stuff. Some is what you might call questionnaire information, but I didn't want to leave anything out. My questionnaire information might not be your questionnaire information. I'll email you the file, too. If I remember more stories, I'll email you these too. But I think I have them all.
- Caris

P.S. I'm worried about your grandmother. I suggested a weekend trip, thinking it would help her to get away from Dale. She would not even consider a one-night trip. Maybe your grandmother will be more likely to listen to you. Take a weekend, or even a night, off to be with her if you can.

Lena thumbed through the sheets. Fifty pages, double spaced Times New Roman, 12-point font.
You shouldn't have, Caris.
The first story started:

Dale and I went to Nanjing, a Chinese restaurant, for our first date. (Side note: The health department closed Nanjing the next day. I've always wondered if the chicken that tasted "off" was really rat.) Okay, maybe technically it wasn't a date. She had asked me out so I could give her tips on how she could better land clients—what her nervous tics were, etc. In any case, it wasn't the best outing. Our conversation didn't flow.
Near the end of dinner, though, we got to talking about personal stuff.

She mentioned she'd been married. Her husband died of AIDS when their daughter was very young.

The change in Dale was immediate. She went from a somewhat aloof lawyer to soft and glowing. "My daughter is like her father," Dale said. "Thank goodness. But she takes after me in some not-so-good ways."

"What was your husband like?" I asked. I was surprised. I'd thought she was gay. Certainly looked it.

She looked at me in this piercing way. "Do you believe in soul mates?"

"Not really."

"Me either. But Reggie was the kind of person who made me believe in soul mates. I miss him every day. I don't remember his voice anymore." She teared up. "He was the sweetest man. I'd marry him again today if I could." She chuckled self-consciously. "And I'm gay and was not attracted to him sexually, so that's saying a lot."

When Dale asked me if we could have dinner again, I almost said no. She was older. Too old for me, or so I thought. Her daughter was my age. But my gut told me to give it another try. This was a complex woman, a woman who knew how to love. So I said yes.

*****

Caris got a letter from Lena a few days later.

Caris:

Thank you for the binder. You shouldn't have, but I really appreciate it. I got this weekend off from work. I had to beg and switch shifts with a few people, but I got it done. I'll use that to guilt-trip Grandma into going somewhere. You're right that she needs a break from Mom.

Anyway, I went to a wedding yesterday: Deonte Stallings' wedding. In case you do not remember, Deonte is Nakeem and Aron's biological father. The wedding was nice. I think I was the only white person there. I should've asked you to come with me. Don't know why I didn't. I've missed you.

Well, anyway, it's funny how relationships develop, isn't it? At the reception, Deonte's brother said that when Deonte was born, he was so ugly his mama asked the doctor to put him back in. Nervous laughter followed. Nervous because Deonte used to be this—okay, I'll be honest— the joke had some basis in truth. Now he's this strapping handsome guy.

So I was fifteen and at a party. Eager and nervous and excited about getting drunk. Which happened quickly. Four beers, I was wasted. But I didn't stop there. I had a couple of shots.

All white faces. I went to a private high school. Then there was one black face. He was by himself in a corner outside. What I noticed, what impressed me, was the fact he had oodles of beer cans around him. I went up to him, and we had a few cans. His head did not fit his body, which was like a toothpick. Maybe I took his hand, or maybe he took mine, he doesn't remember either, and going upstairs and getting a bedroom, I remember him inside me for maybe thirty seconds, didn't take him long. I thought: "Hey this doesn't hurt like people said it would." And I remember going to throw up.

It hurt in the morning. Hell yes it did.

Deonte went to a public high school. No reason I should have seen him again. But, of course, I was pregnant. So because of that thirty seconds he was inside me, can you believe that, not even a minute, not even a freaking minute, Deonte Stallings and I have a strange, lifelong relationship, and I went to his wedding.

I hope to get married someday. Wonder if Deonte will be at my wedding. I hope Nakeem, Aron, Malik and Joanna are too. Here's what I really wonder, though: Will Deonte and I be invited to Nakeem's and Aron's weddings? I hope so. I really do.

Thank you again for the binder. I've read everything. I'll call you very soon. I've missed you. Let's get together so we can maybe get naked or whatever. Or not naked. Just, you know. Whatever.

-Lena

Chapter 17

"No," Shirley said.

"No?" Lena replied. "Grandma, I cleared my weekend for you. Do you know how hard that was? I got—"

"I never asked you to do that."

"You want to do this the hard way, fine. I'll get handcuffs and swallow the key. I'll get chloroform. I'll invent a time travel machine, go back in time, get a black belt and ninja you to the ground. I'll get a crowbar and knock you out and drag you to my car. You *are* going out of town with me this weekend, and we're going to have fun. Capisce?"

Shirley permitted a teeny smile. "Te ragazza testarda."

"What?"

"Italian for 'you stubborn girl.' "

"You know Italian?"

"I know 'you stubborn girl' in many languages. I used to say it all the time to Dale when she was a child. Threw her off. Got her to be quiet for a few minutes."

"Smart."

Shirley sighed and glanced at Dale. "All right, Lena. All right. You and Caris win. I surrender. Peacefully. No chloroform necessary."

"Great."

"I've been wanting to spend time with Donovan, anyway. I miss giving him his bottle."

"Caris is coming?"

Shirley cocked an eyebrow. "Isn't she?"

"She, uh, yeah, sure. I'll give her a call." *A weekend with Caris? And Donovan and Grandma? Could be torture. Or could be...* Lena refused to finish the thought. She would call Caris, they would agree it was for the best if she did not go on the trip, Caris could feign being sick at the last minute, and that would be that.

Or was that childish? Lena and Caris were adults. What was the big deal if Caris came? They could act fine and stiff and distant around each other. *Right. Right.*

*****

"So," Lena said, "what do you think?"

Joanna Soundros nodded her approval. "It's fine. Cute little place. Where will my daughter sleep?"

"She can sleep in my bed, and I'll sleep in the living room. Or vice versa. I won't make Aron sleep in the kitchen sink."

Joanna did not laugh.

"I appreciate this," Lena said. "Thank you."

"I'm not doing it for you."

"I know."

"She got her period last month. First time."

"Ick," Lena said.

"She might be on it when she stays with you."

"All right. Just let me know. What kind of pads does she use? Or tampons?"

Joanna answered the question and then held out her hand. "Goodbye, Lena."

Lena took Aron's mother's hand. "Bye, Joanna." She hated the distance between her and Joanna. They had used to be so close. The frost was Lena's fault, of course. Lena was the one who stopped coming to see the children. The one who stopped answering phone calls. The one who was off presumably enjoying a fresh new life in college. The one who jumped into Europe for three years and brought back nary a souvenir.

Lena walked Joanna to her car. "I'll be out of town this weekend with family. Cell service is spotty where I'm going to be. In case you call and can't get in touch."

Joanna smiled coolly. As if to say: *Like I'd call.*

*****

Lena was behind the wheel for the nearly four-hour drive to the Peaks of Otter lodge in Bedford County, Virginia. The ride down was awkward in some ways. Lena felt as invisible ice were separating her and Caris. She wanted to reach out and touch Caris. Kiss her. Hold her.

In other ways, the ride was not bad. Shirley taught Lena and Caris how to say "you stubborn girl" in twelve languages.

"I hope Donovan doesn't mind being called a girl, even if it's in another language," Caris said with a laugh.

They arrived about eight o'clock and checked in. The nearby National D-Day Memorial was having an event, so the lodge was booked. The four of them would share one room; Lena would have to put up with Shirley's snores. And put up with Caris being so close, yet so far.

At the lodge restaurant, they took a table by the window, with a view of the man-made lake and Flat Top, one of the mountains for hiking.

"You girls should hike tomorrow," Shirley said. "I'll watch Donovan."

"Sure," Lena said, looking out the window. The prospect of being alone with Caris caused her pussy to tingle and her heartbeat to quicken. A stolen, sweaty encounter in the woods…

Dusk gradually turned over to night. The lake's waters were placid and still. Lena figured that most people would perceive peacefulness and serenity. Not her. She saw her mother's blank, lifeless eyes. She shuddered, wanting to banish the thought. "Excuse me. I'm going to the bathroom." She made her way across the dining room and headed downstairs.

She splashed cold water on her face and studied her reflection in the mirror. What was this? A lake, her mother's eyes? *Chin up. Go back to the beautiful woman waiting for you. The beautiful woman you're scared of.*

*****

After dinner, they went for a walk around the lake. Shirley, Caris and Lena took turns pushing Donovan. There were no night lights, although the moon afforded some visibility.

"I should call Pinewood before we go back to our room," Shirley said after one lap around the lake.

"Pinewood has the number. They'll call if something happens," Lena pointed out.

"What if they lost the number?"

"All right, Grandma. You're right. Call and check on Mom."

"This trip was a bad idea," Shirley said.

Caris took her hand. "Shirley, it—"

"What if Dale has a stroke and I'm not there, or—"

"She's fine," Caris said.

"She has another urinary tract infection."

"And it'll go away smoothly like the others did," Lena put in.

"You think I like this?" Shirley asked. Her eyes, glowing and accusing, studied Caris and Lena. "Well, do you? You think I like being like this? I'm pathetic. I know it. I drove away my husband. But she's my daughter. She's part of me."

Lena did not know what to say. Neither did Caris, apparently, because she kept quiet. "Look. Deer," Lena said. Four deer within arms' length, looked like two does and two fawns. "Hey," Lena whispered. "Used to people, are you? Come here." She took a tiny step toward the deer, and they ran off. *Oh well.* Lena glanced up at the sky. "It's a nice night. We don't get this in Alexandria."

"I'm going to call Pinewood," Shirley said. "See you back at the room."

Lena's stomach knotted as Shirley retreated.

"She's right," Caris whispered. "This trip was a bad idea. I should've known this would happen."

"I thought maybe once we were out of town, she would...I don't know. Get drunk on the fresh air or something."

Caris laughed. "The fresh air here is very low in alcoholic content."

"I missed hearing your laugh."

Caris's smile increased a little. "Yeah?"

"Mmm."

"La!" Donovan.

Lena reached down and hauled him up. Perhaps as a natural barrier between her and Caris. He was heavy. "Damn. Has he gained a hundred pounds?"

Another laugh from Caris, deeper.

"I'm ready for Mom to die," Lena said, the abruptness surprising her. "I'm tired of this waiting. This limbo. Is that horrible?"

"Of course not," Caris said quietly.

"It's what Grandma needs, too. To move on with her life."

"The deer are back," Caris said.

"We gonna hike tomorrow?"

"I guess so."

Lena placed Donovan back in his stroller. "I'm nervous."

"About what? The hike?" Caris's voice was soft. Husky.

"Yes. And Aron's staying with me next Friday night."

"That's great, Lena."

"Not sure what to do, but I'll figure it out. I'll let Aron take the lead."

"You should tell your grandmother about Aron and Nakeem."

"So she has another problem?"

A bemused smile curved Caris's lips, and Lena could resist her no longer. She pressed her mouth to Caris's, let Caris part their lips, let Caris's tongue caress hers.

"What was that for?" Caris said afterward.

"Drunk on fresh air."

Caris kissed her again.

"I'm sorry I'm an idiot," Lena said.

"Shh. You're not an idiot."

"I've been avoiding you."

Caris laughed. "I've been avoiding you too."

"I want, uh, I've been wanting—I'm a little tired of, uh, I'd like to see you, Caris. All of you. Naked. You asked before if we could do naked sometime. Can we, soon? Very soon?"

"Please. Yes. Please."

*****

None of the rooms at the lodge had a TV. Or a phone, although there were a few banks of pay phones. The lodge emphasized getting away from the hustle and bustle of everyday life. Cellphone reception was poor. The rooms did not have refrigerators either, and Caris had brought a small one to keep Donovan's milk in.

Caris put Donovan to bed. She joined Lena and Shirley on the back deck of their room. They sat on a wicker couch with Shirley in between Caris and Lena. The couch cushion was so thin it did no good, but to offset that discomfort, they had a gorgeous view of the lake, and above them, the smooth silhouette of Flat Top.

She, Lena and Shirley were silent, but around them, frogs croaked, fireflies lit up, an occasional deer wandered by, and once in a while, a child shrieked. Overall, it was calm. Peaceful.

Shirley broke the silence. "What do you look for in a woman?"

Caris stirred. She had been falling asleep. "Are you asking me?"

Shirley shrugged. "You and Lena."

"I'll let Lena go first."

"Nothing specific," Lena began thoughtfully, and Caris stared at the Flat Top silhouette. "I try to avoid preconceived ideas or notions. But in general, honesty. Humor. Kindness. An open mind. A spark of, I don't know, drive. I look for a woman who wants to live, who wants to make a difference. Who isn't afraid to fight injustice. A woman for whom money isn't everything. I'm not like Mom. I don't like fancy jewelry. I'd be happier with an engagement ring from one of these little machines that look like gumball machines. Boy, okay. I guess I can get pretty specific. Or not. I don't know. I don't look for anything. There's either a spark and click, or there isn't. Someone who doesn't mind listening to me ramble."

"You ramble just right," Shirley said.

"Thanks," Lena replied with a laugh. "Hey, Grandma. What do you look for in a guy?"

"Art."

"Art?"

"Art. Creativity. Soul. Do you know how your grandfather and I met?"

"No."

Caris closed her eyes to relax into the story. "I was seventeen years old, at a street fair with my best friend. Your grandfather was there, with

113

his father, but not to have fun. They were working. They did drawings, like portraits. Not caricatures, just portraits, beautiful portraits. If you paid five cents extra, they did the drawings in color."

"Granddad draws?"

"Beautifully. He's drawn many pictures of you, Lena. He has a little book at home, a pocket notebook type with blank pages, and that's the Lena book. Anyway, my friend, Marjorie, thought your granddad was cute. I thought his ears were too big, but I humored Marjorie. We sat individually for our drawings. Marjorie fussed about her picture, but when I looked at my drawing, I..." Shirley inhaled a dreamy, tremulous sigh. "He'd *seen* me. He'd *understood* me. Captured me. He'd drawn the real me. I went back the next day and asked his name. George Philip Carter III."

"Why didn't Granddad—I mean—his drawings? Why didn't he hang them or...? Why did he work as a salesman?"

"He never realized how good he was. Plus he was scared to try. To *really* try."

"That's sad," Caris said.

"Yes. Absolutely. So, what about you? What do you look for in a woman? Obviously, you like older women."

Caris grinned. "Well, I married an older woman, but I don't have a type. Whatever happens happens. Were you surprised when you found out how young I was?"

"Of course I was," Shirley said. "But you can't control love."

"No," Caris murmured. "You can't."

"Can we go back tomorrow afternoon?"

"Sure, Grandma," Lena said. "If that's what you want."

"This place is nice. Peaks of Otter. Really nice. I appreciate you girls thinking of me." Shirley let out a sigh. "But I need to go back."

*****

Flat Top was touted as a strenuous, three-mile round-trip trek. The September morning was about sixty-five degrees and would feel much hotter after Caris and Lena got into their hike. They wore shorts and T-shirts. Their plan after the hike was to shower, eat at the lodge and head home. Caris liked hiking—the sweat, the outdoors, the sheer determination of pressing ahead, focusing only on moving.

At the top, green mountains surrounded her and Lena—and the fifteen or so other people scattered about.

"There's the lodge." Lena pointed toward the hotel and the lake.

"They look like toys."

"We've come a long way."

Have we really?

"I didn't like being in the cot last night," Lena said.

"You should've slept in the bed with me."

Lena snorted. "I couldn't have."

Caris had had a dream last night. The same dream every night since Monday, actually. The endings varied, but the beginning and the middle were the same. She and Lena were at a beach, lounging in the sand. Lena wore a red string bikini. Caris wore a black bikini. "Time for more sun block," Caris said.

Lena undid her top and revealed a pair of luscious breasts. Caris gently kissed each nipple. "On your stomach."

"Mmmm." Lena rolled over.

Caris kissed Lena's back and squeezed a trail of sun block on it. Sometimes, when Lena rolled back over, she was Dale, grinning, grabbing Caris, sticking her tongue in Caris's mouth. "Can't you kiss?" Dale would growl.

Another ending had the face being Shirley's. She would still kiss Caris, be just as hostile. Sometimes the person turned out to be Caroline. The person never was Lena.

Out of the corner of her eye, Caris studied Lena. She was drenched in sweat, and the washcloth she pressed to her forehead made hardly a dent. Caris's chest constricted. For a minute, she was breathless, and her whole being hurt. Unfortunately, this was not their time. Their time would never come. They would get naked. They would make love.

Still would not be their time.

"I'm hot," Lena grumbled. "Men are lucky. They can take their shirts off, no problem."

"You should be fine in your sports bra."

Lena elbowed Caris in the ribs. "Trying to get me to take my shirt off?"

"I'm trying to get you to take all your clothes off."

Lena rested her head against Caris's shoulder. "How about tonight? Come be with me tonight."

Chapter 18

"Oh, Lord." Jennifer's jaw dropped when Caris walked down the steps that night. "You look amazing. I want to dry hump you to kingdom come."

Caris laughed. She was wearing the black dress and was beginning to like her breasts exactly the way they were. Their voluptuousness. The dress was perfect for fucking with clothes on, if she and Lena decided to backtrack and go that route.

Caris's body was already reacting. Imagining Lena mounting her on the loveseat, or her mounting Lena, Lena moaning and rocking her hips. The sweat on Lena's forehead, on her neck.

Caris's mother had a date, so Caris had tried to find a neighborhood baby sitter. She could not on such short notice. Lena could come to the townhouse, but Caris did not want the risk of Donovan crying. She also wanted some time to herself after sex. Besides, all-night lovemaking if Lena came to the townhouse might be too perilous. So, last resort: Jennifer. She hated lying to Jennifer. Had told Jennifer on the phone that she had a blind date, set up through someone she kept in touch with from the temp job.

"I'll be back by eleven." Caris was due at Lena's apartment at eight.

"So does this mean you weren't too crazy about Patricia? I thought you liked her. She really liked you."

"I did. I do. She's nice. I'm exploring the sea."

"Scuba dive safely."

Caris grinned. "I will. Call the cell if you need me." She gave her best friend a hug. "Bye."

Depersonalize the experience as much as you can. You'll be fine.

*****

When Caris laid eyes on Lena, Caris felt her resolve to be steely and impersonal jump a train and choo off. Because Lena looked miserable. No, not miserable. Nervous. A volcano of nerves primed to erupt.

Caris did enjoy Lena's sharp intake of breath and the gaze that struggled to stay above bust level.

"You can look," Caris said teasingly.

"I'm a gentlewoman. An underdressed gentlewoman." Lena indicated her jeans.

Caris leaned in for a quick, feathery kiss on Lena's cheek, a kiss that she hoped did not mask her nervousness too much. She wanted to convey to Lena that they were in this together.

"When's the last time you had sex?" Caris asked. "Other than what we've done. Because these weren't really — anyway. So when's the last time?" Lena smelled like raspberry strawberry blueberry whatever. Relaxing, subtle.

A surprised blink from Lena. "Before the, with the, before the wreck. With Caroline. I'm clean. Is that why you asked?"

"I asked because I'm nervous. Really nervous. You're so lovely. So beautiful. I want to impress you. I don't know if I will." Caris thought of the stretch marks, the milk that might leak.

Lena snorted. "You think you're nervous? All I can think about is you comparing me and Mom and what if I'm not as good as — " She stopped abruptly, pink flushing her cheeks.

"All I can think about is you, you, you. Nothing else. No one else," Caris said. "Please believe me."

Lena searched her face. Believing her, but the scrutiny was impaling. Erotic, too. "Want me to light a candle? Candles?" Lena asked.

"Okay."

Nervous words trickled forth. "Or incense? I like incense better. Well, for the smell. For this, candles might be better. They're nice. Incense can give off a lot of smoke. Might ruin the mood. Sometimes the shadows candles cast are cool."

"Candles are fine," Caris said, but she felt like someone else had lassoed her tongue and was talking for her. *We're actually going to do this.*

Lena got candles from the kitchen and led Caris into the bedroom. Her blinds and curtains were down, and the room was semi-dark. Lena set the candles on her dresser and lit them. They were hot, leaping orange flags.

"Cinnamon," Lena explained. "Not the most romantic, but all I had. Thought I had more."

"I love cinnamon."

Lena clapped her hands together with a vigorous efficiency. "Anyway, do you want the lights off? Would that make you more comfortable? Do you want to wait until it gets really dark outside?"

"No, just maybe the lamp on to start with."

Lena tapped the lamp on to its lowest setting and turned the main light off. "What do you like?" she asked.

"What do I like?"

"In bed. What would you like me to do?"

"Surprise me."

Lena inclined her head jerkily. "You gonna surprise me, too?"

"I can."

Lena reached for her. Slipped her hands up Caris's arms, ever so slowly, and then Lena's lips were on her neck. Lena's breath tickled. Her mouth was soft, soothing, and left a series of slow and shivery kiss-nibbles. Gooseflesh rippled across Caris's arms, her legs, her stomach.

She moaned.

Lena, of all people, was kissing Caris's neck, was asking Caris what she wanted.

No surprises. Clothes on. "I really enjoy, uh…I don't know what'll happen if you play with my nipples. I don't nurse anymore, but milk might leak."

"I bet I'm cute with a milk mustache. Milk does a body good."

"If you had a milk mustache, I could lick it off."

"Mmm." Lust deepened Lena's reply.

Clothes on. Clothes on. Caris wrapped her arms around Lena's waist, enjoying the feel of Lena's hips and stomach. "Are your legs tired? You've been running through my mind all day."

Lena chuckled. "That's terrible."

"Lots more terrible where that came from. If I could rearrange the alphabet, I would put U and I together."

"That one's a little better."

Clothes on. "So what do you like?" Caris asked, hating how her voice was apprehensive. Anxious. She really wanted to please Lena. Liked Lena so much. Wanted to convey how much she appreciated Lena helping her.

But she would try her damnedest to convey the sentiment with her black dress on.

"You're sweet," Lena said.

"Sweet on you."

"So you like your breasts to be touched," Lena said.

"Yes. Pinched. Nibbled. Fondled. Sucked. Whatever. Are you gonna tell me what you like?"

"Most everything."

"You like alien probes?"

"My favorite. Even more than a hot rod up my ass."

"I brought several hot rods and no alien probes."

"We can use the hot rods, don't worry." Lena kissed the tip of Caris's nose, then her eyelids and then her earlobes. "I like you. I like you a lot, Caris. I like kissing you. I like a whole lot of things. I like watching people touch themselves. I like penetrating my lover and having my lover penetrate me, maybe at the same time. With a dildo, finger, tongue, whatever. Having people go down on me, and vice versa. And I—I like you, Caris. I will love whatever we do. Clothes on, no kissing on the mouth, alien probes, stun guns, grenades, space invaders, green goo, Martians, whatever. Long as I'm with you."

Damn Lena for being so sweet. Caris was *thisclose* from tugging Lena to her and kissing her. Kissing her all night.

*****

Caris went to get water. "Do you have dildos?" she asked when she returned.

"Yes." Lena bent to get her stash of sex toys from the nightstand drawer. She rained the contents of her bag onto the bed. Lube. Four dildos, two straps, the baker man vibrator and one other vibrator. A feather. Handcuffs. "Mostly remnants from when I was with Caroline," Lena offered helpfully. Furthering the cause of Plan B.

"That one." Caris indicated a purple silicone dildo. "Put it on."

"You want me to just, like, move and uh…can you come like that?"

"I need to be on top."

Lena chewed the inside of her lip. *This is not going to work.* "Forget the dildo for a minute." Lena wrapped her arms around Caris. "We'll be okay, Caris. We really will."

"I know."

"Let me kiss you."

They kissed leisurely, entwining their arms and legs. Letting their hips find each other and start a familiar dance.

Lena could tell that Caris was still holding back. Still struggling to not let herself go completely, struggling not to lose herself in a whirlwind of passion and sensations.

But Caris was losing, badly. And coming to terms with it. Her kisses grew more daring. Hungrier. No holds barred. Lena melted against Caris, and the world was her and this woman.

*****

Caris watched as Lena tugged the black dress off, then tugged off her own clothes. Lena's breasts were perfect globes, with erect light pink peaks. Dainty nipples. Exquisite.

Caris drew in a breath. "Oh," she whispered.

"Like what you see? Told ya they got better."

Caris wriggled her fingers. "I'm a kid in a candy store." She ventured a touch and a few nibbles. "You're beautiful, Lena. I'm going to sound like a broken record, but you are. Beautiful, beautiful, beautiful. Lovely. The kind to inspire a library of badly written poetry."

Lena laughed. "Wow. I'll have to remember that. So beautiful I inspire a library of badly written poetry."

Caris tugged Lena onto the bed, and Caris's mouth led her to the trimmed patch of dark hair between Lena's legs.

Lena arched her head back and shuddered.

Caris tasted her. "You're a river."

"A river named Caris."

"You taste good."

"You have a fantastic body."

"You're a fantastic liar." Caris hoped her tone signaled that she knew Lena meant every word.

Lena pulled Caris back up and rolled atop her. She kissed Caris's stomach and ran her tongue over the light stretch marks. "I'm not lying. If you had a perfect body, you'd be boring."

Caris grinned. "So you admit I was boring before."

"You were snoozeville. Zzzzz. Is it any wonder I used to avoid you?"

"Then you're terrifically boring. Because your body is, I...I...I don't mean I'm shallow. I only mean that...maybe I should shut up because I don't know what I'm saying."

Lena brought herself to Caris's mouth for another long kiss with lots of tongue. They were skin to skin, nipples to nipples. Caris abandoned herself to the whirl of sensation, let Lena see her face, let Lena feel her, her moans, groans, cries, expressions of torture, of ache, of need.

The next couple of hours were one of the best, if not the best, of Caris's life. She and Lena came separately and together, their lovemaking more on the side of sweet and exploratory, lots of kissing, than mad animal lust.

But they had mad animal lust in them too, oh yes they did. They had so much potential, and Caris could not wait to experience everything.

She hoped she would get to.

*****

"You had sex," Jennifer said when Caris got home.

"What?"

"That's a sex flush on your neck. Blind date, my ass. More like a booty call." A mischievous grin. "Who is it?"

The lie came easily. Too easily. "No one you know."

Maybe Caris should feel guilty about the lie. Maybe her head should hurt. Maybe mortification should be snaking around her heart. So what? She did not care what she had done, why she had done it. She might later, but in this minute, she was happy. She would make no apology for her feelings.

Jennifer, her gaze eager, tugged Caris to the couch. "So? Tell me about her. What's she like?"

Caris had to say *something*. Get it off her chest. "She scares me."

Jennifer frowned. "Huh?"

"My feelings for her scare me. I've never felt like..." Caris swallowed. "She's really sweet. Funny. Gorgeous as all hell. We connect, we really do. She doesn't expect anything from me. She accepts me for who I am. Stretch marks and big tits and Dale and Donovan and all. That by itself is scary enough. But there's just something about us together that..." Caris gestured vaguely. "It's scary. Also one of the best feelings. I didn't expect this to happen. And so soon after Dale. And the baby."

"Think you're on the rebound?"

"Could be. My body playing tricks on me. My heart playing tricks on me."

Jennifer's eyes narrowed. "Is she taking advantage of you?"

"No way. Anyway, there's no future for us. We both know that. Maybe that's why I feel the way I do, because she's safe. So I'm giving myself permission to...oh, I don't know."

"Why is there no future?"

"I don't want a relationship. Not for a long while." *And not with my wife's daughter.*

"What's her name?"

"I need..." Caris pictured Lena rubbing her own cheek. Lena thinking. Lena stalling.

"I know her, don't I?"

"No."

"It's a man."

Caris snorted. "Sure."

"It's a man. You're seeing a man."

Caris rolled her eyes. "I'm seeing a woman. A wonderful, lovely woman."

Chapter 19

The next morning, Caris and Donovan headed to Pinewood. Dale's room was empty. "She's outside with Shirley," Joe said.

Caris found them at the banks of the duck pond: Dale in her wheelchair and Shirley on a bench under weeping willows. Good spot in the shade.

Shirley took the baby from Caris. "Your grandma says hi!" Shirley chirped.

Something was off about Shirley, despite her apparent cheer. She did not have the somewhat manic vibe she had developed after Dale's wreck.

"You okay?" Caris asked. *Missing George, maybe?*

Shirley pursed her lips. "Are you going to wear your rings again?"

Caris studied her bare fingers. "No."

"Dale hurt you too much." Matter-of-fact voice.

"Yes."

"I'm sorry."

"Me too," Caris murmured.

"That cloud," Shirley said. "What do you think it is?" She indicated the sole cloud in the sky.

Caris saw a shell and a head poking out. Four little feet. "A turtle."

Shirley laughed. "That's what I thought, too." She squeezed Caris's hand and let go. "What's going to happen when Dale wakes up? She can't get her heart broken. It'd put her rehab back years."

"She was leaving me," Caris said. "She'd already resigned herself to the fact we were over."

"You know for sure she was leaving you?"

"Yes."

"It's good of you to visit."

"She was my wife. I loved her. She was supposed to be Donovan's mother."

"Do you think she's waking up?"

"I don't know," Caris said. "I look at her and I find it hard to believe she might. But other people have woken up." *Shirley, she's not waking up. I'm sorry.* Caris knew in her heart Dale was not waking up. Dale was dead. Caris would not be with Lena otherwise. Period.

Shirley rubbed her forehead, and the energy she had absorbed from Dale over the past months seeped out. Shirley looked her age now. Then some. "What are you going to do if my daughter wakes up?"

Caris opened her mouth. Closed her mouth. First time Shirley had said if, not when. "I have no idea, Shirley. I'll be at her side, if she wants me. But not as her wife. I'm not going to be part of her second chance." Caris cleared her throat. "Shirley, I've started dating again. Nothing serious. But I'm dating."

Shirley gazed out to the pond. "Dating. I see. I woke up this morning and called for George." She chuckled wryly. "Took me a moment to remember he'd gone." She sniffled. "We're eighty-two. Too old for this. What if he forgets to take his heart pills?"

Caris snaked an arm around Shirley. *Lena, Lena, Lena. I think I love you, Lena. No, you don't.* Desperation for affection and contact is driving this. Don't dare think you love her.

The twittering of birds brought Caris back to the present. "I was going to contest the living will," Shirley was saying. "I'm not anymore. My daughter wouldn't have wanted this. I'm beginning to think George is right. Dale is gone. She's dead."

"Perhaps."

"Caris," Shirley said.

"Hmm?"

"I'm not blind. I see what's happening between you and Lena."

The sentence was a jolt in Caris's body. "Nothing is—"

"I'm not blind," Shirley repeated. "I knew right away when I saw how Lena was dressed that night you went bowling. That girl, bless her heart, *never* dresses up. I've tried to pretend, tried to stay out of it. I can't anymore. I don't like it. It's disrespectful."

"Shirley, I—no. Nothing's—Shirley, Lena went bowling from work."

"Lena wears that green skirt to work, or jeans and T-shirts," Shirley retorted. "Please don't make me recite how else I—it would best if you didn't come here anymore. If you didn't spend time with me anymore. Or Lena, for that matter."

Caris tensed her hand, still on Shirley's shoulder. "Shirley," Caris said. "Please don't do this. You're like a mother to me, and—"

"I didn't do anything," Shirley said. "You did it. I don't know how far it's gone, and I don't want to know."

"It's not like that."

"Stop. Please just stop."

"We were going to end it soon."

"I don't want to hear any more." Shirley stood and pushed Dale away.

*****

123

In the parking lot, Caris secured Donovan in his car seat and slumped into her own seat. Her chest was like cement.

Crap.

Crap.

Was Shirley going to talk to Lena? Probably not. Lena was her granddaughter, her flesh and blood. Best to blame the outsider, the daughter-in-law. The blond vixen. Certainly not her own secretive, emotionally distant, emotionally abusive daughter.

Maybe Caris should have told Shirley about Dale being transgender and how that had brought Caris and Lena closer. Maybe that—*no, it would have made matters worse.* Bottom line was, there was a reason Lena and Caris were afraid to articulate they had relationship potential. Maybe they were not having an affair, per se, but they were sneaking behind people's backs. They felt like their connection was wrong, illicit. Hell, Caris had not been able to tell Jennifer, her own best friend, about Lena.

Caris hated how she had hurt Shirley.

She hated how she herself could not stop thinking about Lena. Lena's smile, Lena's laugh. Lena's nipples and pussy in Caris's mouth.

Then Dale's blank expressions.

When Caris got home, she retrieved her rings from the jewelry box. She slipped them on one last time. Light caught the diamond, giving it an unearthly shine, as if it knew its last breath had arrived.

"Goodbye, Dale," Caris whispered. She knew what she would do with the rings. She would bury them with her wife.

*****

The Pleasure Place was much the same as Caris remembered from her most recent trip, about two years ago. The sex shop was one of several in DuPont Circle, Washington, D.C.'s gay and lesbian district.

Lena held Donovan as Caris maneuvered his stroller down the steps into the store. With the cashier's permission, Caris left the stroller behind the front counter, and she and Lena started looking. The store was on the small side and five people, four of them men, meandered about.

"Your baby is adorable," a man wearing a rainbow tie-dye shirt told Lena.

Her cheeks flushed. "He—he's not mine. I mean, uh, he's my bro—thank you."

The man smiled and walked off.

"No big deal," Caris whispered. She took her son. Donovan was sleepy; his eyes kept opening and closing. "So. See anything you like? I like silicone better."

"Me too."

Caris was not sure why she was at the store. Lena had suggested it; Caris should have told her right then that Shirley knew. But Caris was not ready just yet to say goodbye to Lena.

They settled on a double penetration dildo, a regular purple silicone dildo and a harness but kept looking at other merchandise, such as handcuffs, lube and costumes. "I'm horny," Lena muttered. "Didn't think I could get any hornier, but I am."

"Me too," Caris said, although she was not. She felt hollow and stiff, like an arthritic tin man.

"Ever done it in public?"

"Once. Semi-public. On a racquetball court at the gym."

"Come on," Lena whispered.

Caris and Lena paid for their purchases, and Lena led them to the Starbucks across the street. She locked the bathroom door behind them. Donovan was asleep, and Caris positioned his stroller so that he was facing the wall.

Lena pulled Caris's pants down and got on her knees. Caris shoved Shirley out of her mind and let Lena work her magic.

*****

They had an early dinner at the DuPont Italian Kitchen. "Want to come to the house tonight after you finish work? We can break in the dildos," Caris said.

Lena returned her lover's smile. "You read my mind." She wanted to tell Caris many things: how Caris made her feel alive, so unlike anything that had come before. That what she had with Caris paled to everything else, that she could stare at Caris for hours on end and kiss her for hours on end, too.

Lena said nothing. That would never unfold. She could not imagine telling her grandparents, who were just about the only family she had left, that she was screwing their daughter's wife.

"Donovan's teething," Caris warned. "He's going to cry."

"I'll get him if he cries. No problem."

Caris replied with a tense smile.

I'll get him if he cries. Bzzz! Wrong answer, Lena. No need to telegraph how much you like Caris. You're not supposed to be that easy about the kid.

*****

125

They made love after Lena finished work, the same dildo in both of them. Caris was on top first, and when Lena's turn came, she straddled Caris. Cupped Caris's cheeks in her hands and left them there as their bodies moved. Her stare was bold and assessed Caris frankly.

Caris wanted to look away but could not. Lena was reaching into her very soul, reading and caressing it.

Lena knew they were right together, too. Caris was sure of it. *Lena is in love with me. Head over heels in love with me, just like I'm with her. This shouldn't be happening. We're supposed to be passing ships.*

Passing ships.

She's supposed to want nothing to do with Donovan.

Lena's expression scared her. Her own feelings for Lena scared her, and no woman had looked at her like this during lovemaking.

Lena moaned, sweat glistening on her forehead. The "mm-nn" moan, unique to Lena, that meant she was close to orgasm. Caris took one of Lena's breasts in her mouth. Their bodies moved in greater harmony, but then Donovan howled.

"Shit," Lena said, but she got him, like she had said she would. She returned with him. "I changed his diaper. Does he need a bottle?"

"Nah."

Lena got into bed with the baby. She lay Donovan on her stomach and studied him. Made faces at him.

She's so good with him, she looks and acts like his mother sometimes, she looks more like his mother than I do, they're natural together...

Remember she doesn't want kids. Big difference between being a parental figure and making faces at him once in a while.

"Why?" Caris asked.

"Why what?"

"Why did you really get these infant-care books from the library?"

"Because I like him. Because he's family. To help you out."

"Okay."

Lena did not meet Caris's gaze. "Didn't mean to freak you out."

"You didn't."

"La la la!" Donovan.

"Maybe we should stop," Caris said. The words were icicles in her own heart.

Lena's expression turned careful. "Stop what?"

"This. Us."

"Why?"

"Your grandmother knows about us. She's upset. I don't want you to lose her."

Lena was silent for a few seconds. So silent and so still Caris was not sure Lena had heard. Then Lena kissed Donovan's nose. Once, twice, three times. "Oh, Caris." Lena sounded like she was going to cry.

"So we should stop," Caris said. "We weren't going anywhere, right? This was what it was. A fling isn't worth the — "

"I get your point," Lena whispered. "I get your freaking point." She continued looking at Donovan. "How does she know?"

"First, she saw the clothes you wore the night we went bowling."

"The — oh, Christ." Lena's tones were angry. Outraged. "You have got to be kidding. Fucking clothes is how she knows?"

"Among other things she wouldn't tell me."

"I should've worn jeans," Lena muttered. "It was stupid of me not to. My fault. Shit."

"Lena, don't. You didn't know you'd be going home with me."

"So she's known since bowling?"

"Apparently."

"Hmm."

"Hmm," Caris echoed.

"Mom really did love you. For what it's worth."

"I really did love her, too." *And I love you.*

"All right," Lena said slowly. "All right. If that's what you want."

"It isn't. It's not what I want at all."

"Not what I want, either."

"So let's talk about us."

Lena got up from the bed. "I'll put him up and go home."

"What about us?"

Lena shook her head. "It's best this way. You know what would happen? Same thing that happens to everyone else. Intense for a while, then a breakup. We're getting it over with now is all. You're right. This isn't any different from Caroline or anyone else. This isn't worth losing family over. Lovers come and go. Family doesn't."

Caris studied her lover's full breasts, nipples pointy and pink, her stomach, her long legs. *We're different, Lena. You know it. I know it.*

Caris said nothing, though. She knew no such thing. Hell, she had probably felt this way at some point with Dale: crazily, dizzyingly, dazzlingly head over heels in love. And look what happened.

"Maybe I'll write you a letter sometime," Lena said.

"I'll reply."

Lena bent down, as if to kiss Caris, but apparently had second thoughts. Lena drew back. "Can we not say goodbye?"

"No goodbye."

Putting Donovan up and going home was exactly what Lena did. Exactly what Caris let her do. No kiss, no goodbye.

Chapter 20

The razor was pink. CVS brand, plastic and disposable, for shaving armpits and legs. Plastic and disposable. Unlike Lena. Caris had been staring at the razor long enough for her bath to go from steaming hot to chilly.

Blood.

Caris blinked and swore. The water bloomed with blood. Must be from a razor nick. Caris was shivering. Her teeth chattered. "Fine," she muttered. She preferred this discomfort to thinking about Lena, who had left an hour ago.

Caris gazed over the blood in the tub. *Right. I'm supposed to be shaving. Instead I'm starting a blood aquarium. How mundane. How boring.* Her heart was numb, so why shouldn't her body be, too? Let the cold do what it wanted. Why was she shaving, anyway? She had no lover or wife to run her hands over her legs, no lover or wife to whisper into her ear.

She and Lena were over. Over, over, over. Caris held her hand up and dropped the razor. It made barely a splash. It was an Olympic diver, graceful, slicing into the water and leaving scant traces of its action. Except it floated. So not like an Olympic diver at all. A pink Olympic log. *I'm going crazy.*

"Yoo-hoo!" Dale's traditional *I'm home* greeting.

Caris jerked upright, then froze.

"Caris, babe? Where are you?"

"B-bathroom," Caris called. *I'm dreaming.* She had fallen asleep in the tub. The time was four-something a.m. This was a dream. Had to be.

Dale came into the bathroom. The Dale with the purple pinstripe suit from the picture of Caris two months pregnant. Dale took one look at the rose-colored water and frowned. "Time for a new bath."

Dale drew a new bath, this time with bubbles. Caris closed her eyes and tried to relax, but the heat of the new water failed to reassure her. Her heart was heavy. She was detached, a Band-Aid pulled off, skin stinging. She floated outside herself, her tub self becoming a statue.

She opened her eyes. Her wife was sitting on the floor. Anxious. Clothed.

Caris, naked.

Caris snorted an acid laugh. "Aren't you dead?"

No answer.

Caris studied her reflection in a bubble. Her face was broad, curved, her eyes ugly blue slants. She stabbed the bubble with her pointer finger. *Pop, you bastard.* The bubble gasped and folded. No pop. Caris chose a bubble that looked compliant and punctured it. She recalled Dale's laugh, Dale's rare but lively, from-the-throat guffaws, the way she took fussy care with her spiky hair and then would look at Caris with vibrant brown eyes and say: "Jesus Lord, Caris, I have the most gorgeous wife in the world. How did I get so lucky?" Whenever Dale picked Caris up in her strong arms and twirled her, Caris felt light and carefree. Now she was nauseated.

"Lena and I can be friends," Caris said. "I've got to try to be there for her, no matter what happened. We're family. She's Donovan's sister."

Dale squeezed body wash on Caris's loofah. "I'll get your back."

"Okay."

As Dale rubbed gentle, relaxing circles, Caris wondered what Lena was doing. Hoped Lena was okay. Relatively okay, anyway.

"I thought she could be the one," Caris whispered.

"You never know. She could be."

Caris turned to her wife. Looked at her. Really looked at her, as if Dale might actually be there instead of being a dream person. Dale's brown eyes were no longer intense. They were warm, liquid, understanding. Caris trailed a finger down Dale's cheek. Smooth cheek. Skin and blood, not mist and imaginings. "Aren't you mad? Me and Lena?"

"Of course I am. But you both did what you had to. I get that. Mom doesn't."

Caris cupped Dale's cheeks and kissed him. "Oh, baby. I love you. I hope you have your second chance now, wherever you are."

*****

Lena had the supplies ready for Aron's visit. No candy or soda — Joanna had said — but popcorn and water was okay. Lena also had a stack of G-rated DVDs and board games. She had Aron from seven p.m. to eleven a.m. Bedtime was at ten p.m., Joanna said, and Aron should not be allowed to sleep past eight a.m. So Lena had her for five waking hours.

Five precious waking hours.

Lena intended to make the best of them.

*****

"So," Lena ventured once Joanna left. "What ya wanna do? I have games, movies and — "

"Can we visit your mom?"

"Now?"

"Yeah."

"No, sweetie. It's late."

"Only seven."

"Still too late."

Aron's gaze was bright. Expectant. "Tomorrow morning?"

"Probably not. I need to talk to your mom first about it."

"Can we visit your stepmother?"

Lena pasted a smile on. *Caris, Caris, oh Caris.* "No, sweetie. I think your mom wanted us to stay here. I should talk to her before taking you to meet anyone."

"What about your friends?"

"Hey! Let's play cards. What games do you know?"

Over Crazy Eights in the living room, Aron asked Lena about her stepmother. "Her name is Caris," Lena said. "She has blond hair. She's — " Lena chuckled. "It's funny. She's about my age. She has a baby. His name is Donovan."

"I like babies."

Lena offered a smile. "Good. Good."

"Could I meet him too?"

"I'll talk to your mom. Promise."

"Can you show me where you work?"

"Um…"

"Please, Lena. Please. Can I see your school too?"

Lena rubbed her forehead. *"Aron, sweetie, why do you…"* Why do you give a fuck about me? Why do you even like me? Why do you take an interest in me?

"What?"

Lena shook her head. She was Aron's mother too, all there was to it. "Okay. All right. I'll show you where I work."

Aron jumped up from the loveseat. "Can we go in?"

"Nope. It's a bar. You have to be twenty-one. Lemme see your driver's license."

Aron giggled. "I'm thirty-one. Reverse thirteen."

Lena got her keys. "Nice try, kiddo."

*****

So they drove to Azizi. Then to George Mason. Then to Pinewood. They stayed in the car everywhere. Aron was full of questions. She wanted to know every detail of Lena's classes, what her job was like, what being at Pinewood was like.

"Can we go by your mom's house?" Aron asked on their way home.

"Okay," Lena whispered, ignoring the voice inside that said such a trip was a bad idea. Because of course Aron would see lights on, would want to go in and meet Caris and Donovan, no matter the time.

Seeing Caris…

Lena wanted to see her. Of course she did. She had ached for Caris. She missed Caris. Regretted leaving Caris. Seeing Caris would be a nice quick little hit. Plus, Lena wanted to show off Aron. Beautiful, intelligent, curious Aron. And Caris was pretty much the only person Lena could show the girl off to.

Lena parked near the townhouse and indicated the place. "Number 349. With the blue shutters."

Lights on. Very much on. At least Aron was quiet. She kept her gaze on the townhouse, her eyes keen and observant. She probably thought the rain gutter was the bee's knees.

Shit. Caris, I love you. I screwed up. It's been an awful week. I could not go to Pinewood. Until tonight, anyway. No way I can get near Grandma.

Lena waited. Five minutes after they parked came the inevitable: "Can we go in, Lena?"

"It's nine o'clock, sweetie."

"Please?"

Lena sighed, giving in. "Let me call my stepmother and see if she's up for visitors."

*****

Caris, her hair hanging long and loose, met them at the door. She wore sweat pants and an old T-shirt. Lena had to fight not to hug her, not to kiss the tantalizing crook of her neck. Instead, Lena placed a hand on Aron's shoulder. "This is Aron." *My daughter.* "She's been wanting to meet you."

Caris's smile was bright, warm and welcoming. But obviously for the child, because Caris had a hard time meeting Lena's gaze. Caris held her hand out. "Hi, Aron. I'm glad you're here. I've been wanting to meet you, too."

The girl's eyes went wide. "You have?"

"Oh yes. Your mother's told me so much about you."

"My mother? You mean Lena?"

Caris blinked. "Right. Sorry."

Aron smiled. "It's okay. She's kind of like my stepmother. Remember, Lena?"

"I remember."

"Well, come in," Caris ushered them into the house.

The next thirty minutes were torture for Lena. She followed Caris and Aron around the house. Caris let Aron peek in on Donovan and give him a kiss, sat on the couch with her and asked the girl about her life, school and friends. They were good together. Beautiful together. Caris was patient and handled Aron's eager questions with grace and good humor.

Only twice did Caris look at Lena—furtive, shy glances. More than enough for Lena to know that she and Caris would end up together someday. They had to. Maybe now was not their time, but their time was coming.

Yes, it was coming.

They would be together.

At nine forty-five, Lena got to her feet. "We gotta go. Bedtime at ten."

"Noooo."

"Yep. Come on."

Aron rolled her eyes. "Fine." She went to the fireplace mantle, apparently for a last look at Lena's high school graduation pictures.

Caris rose as well. "Aron loves you," she whispered.

Lena's chest constricted. "She does?"

Slight, lopsided grin. "She does. Very much. She wants a picture of you."

"She told you that?"

"No. Look at her. Just look at her."

Lena did not want to, not quite, but she forced her gaze to Aron. The girl was tracing the edges of a photo frame.

"She loves you," Caris repeated.

"I love her, too." *Meaning, I love you.*

"I know you do," Caris said softly.

Chapter 21

Two weeks later, Caris started work. She was managing a new branch of Staples. Roses from George arrived at eleven o'clock — *Roses are red, violets are blue, have a great first day at work, dear Caris!*

Shirley must not have told him about Lena.

Caris called him after work to thank him. "How have you been doing?" she asked.

"Not bad. I'm working on a special project. I'm pleased at how it's coming along."

"Oh yeah? What project? Don't leave me in suspense."

He laughed. "You'll see soon enough. I hope."

"Come on."

Another laugh. "Okay, okay. I'm taking an art class. I'm drawing different things, but mostly Dale. I keep seeing her on the boat, the wind in her hair, on her birthday two years ago. I'm trying to capture that. I keep failing, but I'll capture it someday."

"Wow. That's amazing."

"The class has an art show the end of every semester. Maybe you could come up in December for the show."

"I'd love to."

"Maybe you can help me with the drawing of Dale in the boat." George's voice was suddenly somber.

"How can I help you?"

"What was Dale keeping from me and Shirley?"

"What?"

"Dale had a secret. I never asked what it was. Figured that was something best between a mother and daughter. Thing is, I don't know if Shirley noticed. I never told her."

"Oh." Caris glanced around her. She was in her bedroom, on the bed. She saw the walls Dale had painted, the furniture he had picked out. All long before he married her. *George deserves to know. He can handle it.*

"Okay, George," Caris said, and told George about his daughter. Maybe George could capture the real Dale, like he had captured the real Shirley.

*****

133

Betty Crocker turned out to be a decent conversationalist. And her last name was Wilder. Elizabeth Ann "Betty" Wilder. Caris had come into Almond's at the end of her first week at work, hoping to get a buzz and maybe some decent company. The place was busy, and Caris did not see Betty until Betty was standing in front of her.

"Hey," Betty said with a shy smile. "Remember me? You're Melanie Michaels, right?"

Caris shook her head. "Melanie Michaels is my porn star name. I'm Caris. Have a seat. I'll buy you a drink."

After Betty's drink was in place, Betty said that her porn star name was Fluffy Longbottom. "Melanie Michaels is better."

Caris's margarita and her glass of Coke and vodka was taking effect. She leaned into Betty and laughed. "I don't know about that. You can't beat Fluffy Longbottom. So where's the stud?"

"Todd?" Betty wrinkled her nose. "Who knows. You were right. He's an ass. I've been coming here once in a while, looking for you."

Caris met her doe eyes.Not doe eyes anymore, though. "Why looking for me?"

"That kiss. It—it—it changed my life. In a good way. I wanted to thank you. And maybe see if…" Betty did not complete the thought.

"Changed your life how?" *My God. Don't read so much into it. It was just a rash, impulsive act.*

"I had been sleepwalking," Betty said earnestly. "You woke me up."

"Wow."

Betty grinned. "Wow. Yeah. There's this guy—William—who I've been in love with forever. What you did gave me the courage to go up to him and kiss him like you kissed me. He jumped like a giant beetle was attacking him, but whatever. Point is, he knew how I felt. And the agony inside me was gone."

"Good for you."

Betty eyed her speculatively. Closed her hand over Caris's. "What's your story, Melanie Michaels Caris?"

Betty's hand was okay. Felt good. Was not Lena's hand, of course. "My story," Caris muttered. "Where do I start?"

"The beginning?"

Caris squeezed Betty's hand. "Makes sense."

"Let's dance, and you can tell me."

Almond's did not have a dance floor, although soft music played in the background. They got up, and Betty wrapped her arms around Caris. They swayed softly.

"The beginning," Caris said, enjoying Betty's softness. Her plumpness. "I'm in love with my stepdaughter, and she loves me back."

Betty laughed, and Caris did, too.

"You're funny," Betty said.

"Thank you. But I'm serious."

Betty drew back. "Your stepdaughter?"

"Her name's Lena. She's the same age I am. And…" Caris rubbed her cheek. Made her feel closer to Lena.

"Wow," Betty murmured. "Does your partner know?"

"No." *At least, I hope not.*

*****

The next morning, Lena paused in her mother's doorway. Shirley was reading to Dale in the wheelchair. "Tommy proceeded leisurely. By the time he reached the bend of the staircase, he had heard the man below disappear into a back room," Shirley said.

Lena shifted her attention to Dale, who appeared about the same. She wore black sweat pants and an Atlanta Braves T-shirt. That'll be fun. Aron was a New York Mets fan. "All right," Lena whispered. She glanced at Joanna and Aron, who were waiting by the snack machine.

Joanna gave her a little smile, and Lena smiled back. Lena had called Joanna on Thursday night, and they had had an hour-long conversation. A heart to heart. They'd ironed out their issues. Come to a new understanding. Lena had told Joanna that she, Joanna, was the children's mother, period.

Joanna said she knew, but…

There would always be a but, Joanna admitted. However, Joanna said she had always told the children they were special because they had two mommies and daddies. "And, Lena," Joanna added, "I mean it. You gave me two wonderful children. I know it was hard for you and still is. It's hard for me too, but these kids need all four of their parents."

Now, Lena held up her pointer finger and mouthed: "One minute." She'd warned Joanna and Aron that her grandmother would likely be there.

Lena went into the room. "Clearly no suspicion attached to him as yet," Shirley read. "To come to the house and ask for 'Mr. Brown' appeared indeed to be a reasonable and natural proceeding."

"Grandma. Excuse me."

Shirley glanced up. "Lena." She got up and hugged Lena tightly. Lena had not seen her since the Peaks of Otter trip, and if Shirley was angry at Lena for the relationship with Caris, she was not showing it. "Hi, Lena baby."

Lena broke apart from Shirley. "Grandma, I've brought someone to meet Mom. Two someones, actually. They'd like to meet you too."

"Who are they?"

Lena took a deep breath. Her mother had told Shirley about the children. She had to have. "The woman's name is Joanna. The girl's name is Aron. Grandma, she is thirteen years old. She's my daughter."

Shirley did not blink. No surprise. Just a plain, contained face.

"All right, Grandma? I'm going to bring them in."

Shirley swallowed, and her face collapsed for a second. "Yes, yes, please do, dear."

Lena took her grandmother's hand. She studied it, really studied it for the first time. Her hand had character. Experience. Her hand had lived. Shirley wore her wedding ring, a gold band with a small, simple emerald. Her skin was wrinkled. Precious few liver spots, though. She was in good shape. She would live a long time, and Lena was glad. Very glad. Lena brought the hand to her lips and kissed it. "I love you, Grandma."

"I love you too, baby."

Lena brought Shirley out to the hallway. Joanna gave a nervous smile. Aron, an even more nervous smile.

"She's—she's black," Shirley said. "Lena, your daughter is black."

Lena laughed. Laughed so hard tears came to her eyes. She guided Shirley to Aron and Joanna. "This is my grandmother, Shirley," Lena said. "This is Aron, and this is Joanna, her mother."

"Hi, Shirley," Aron said, and Shirley cupped Aron's cheeks in her hands.

"Hello, Aron," Shirley said. "I'm glad to finally meet you. Oh my. You're a beautiful girl, aren't you?"

*****

Caris missed visiting Dale. Well, not visiting Dale per se, but getting away. Pinewood had been like an oasis. A pause in rushed life, where she could slow down, stay as little or as long as she liked, cradle her son and listen to Shirley read.

Instead of going to Pinewood, Caris left Donovan with Phyllis and went to Almond's. She usually met with Betty, who had become a good friend. Jennifer had not asked Caris again about her "mystery" lover, and Caris was glad. She was not sure she could have kept Lena's identity secret. In any case, Caris and Betty never left Almond's together; they were bar friends only. It worked for Caris. She liked being in Betty's arms, letting Betty hold her as they danced. Betty smelled good. Felt good. Was nice and funny. In other circumstances, who knew. Perhaps Caris would have ended up with Betty. However, every time Caris was at to Almond's, she hoped Lena would walk in. This bar was where Lena had used to hang out.

But no Lena.

*****

Aron had taken an instant liking to Agatha Christie. She would be a star someday, that Aron. She did voices and dialogue great. Aron and Joanna visited Pinewood every Wednesday evening from seven to eight, because that was what Aron wanted. Aron and Shirley took turns reading, while Lena and Joanna listened, or more often, worked on a crossword puzzle together. Joanna was dyslexic and had worked hard to overcome it. Lena had not known that about her.

September turned into October, and October into November. Dale had a stroke at the beginning of October. A minor one, the doctors said. The only visible change in her appearance was that the left side of her face drooped a bit. The droop would get worse as time progressed, according to Dale's primary doctor, Peter Aronson. A small blood clot had caused the stroke, he explained, but the stroke had not been as bad as originally feared.

Luckily, he said.

Dale could still blink and move both of her eyes.

Dale had a second stroke, and then another. Dale got more urinary tract infections. And a fourth, tiny stroke. Yet, Dale lived.

*****

George's art debut was at a small gallery fronting the Providence Harbor. Caris, with Donovan in his stroller, walked in fifteen minutes after the show started. She was staying at a hotel; she assumed Lena and Shirley were staying with George.

Many, many groupings of paintings greeted Caris, and she was not sure where to start. Where to find anyone she knew. She wandered around. Most of the work was pretty good. Amateurish, though.

She would be polite with Shirley. More affectionate with George.

With Lena…well. Who knew. The time away from Lena had not dulled Caris's feelings. Lena continued to be on her mind a lot, but Caris was glad Lena had left her alone. That she had left Lena alone. They had needed to get their shit together before they could give themselves to each

137

other. And Caris was almost there. The months had given her enough distance and perspective to realize that her connection with Lena was, indeed, real. Genuine. The connection was more than being caught up in an emotional, charged situation.

However, maybe the time apart had caused Lena's feelings for Caris to dull. The possibility tore Caris in two directions. The first direction: dulled feelings were good. There would be no need to get into a potentially thorny situation. The second direction: oh, no. Caris wanted to be with Lena, ached for Lena to touch her, nibble her, kiss her, look at her. She wanted Lena in her arms, or she in Lena's arms, and have them laugh together. At least an upside existed for whatever direction they were headed for.

Caris felt a touch at her elbow, and then her father-in-law gathered her in for a bear hug. Then he did the same with Donovan.

"You look great," Caris said, and George did. Immersing himself in his art had done wonders. His eyes were vivid, they shone, and he wore a red bowtie.

"You too." They chatted a few minutes, and then George led Caris to his work. "I'm showing twenty-five drawings," he explained.

"Did you get the boat picture right?"

"No," George admitted. "I tried and tried, and then my instructor told me: 'You know what? You can't replicate a perfect moment. So I created another. Tell me what you think. It's Dale waking up. My imagining of it, anyway."

The drawing was titled *Spring* and was the centerpiece. It took up the middle, top to bottom, of one wall. The other pictures, of varying sizes, surrounded Spring.

Caris approached the drawing. Dale's eyes were open, but blank, and Caris's heart fell. *Nothing's changed. George failed.*

Caris did not have the heart to say so, of course. "George, it's very —" Her flesh prickled. From this angle, yes…there was recognition in Dale's eyes. A sparkle. Dale recognizing her. Caris felt Dale call out to her. *Caris! Caris!* A grin struggled to break free from Dale's lips, but she was too weak. She looked like she was grimacing instead. Caris inched toward her. Probably if this was the real Dale, she would smell good, no longer like nursing home. Someone would have sprayed cologne on her. She was becoming a person again. A person who would want her wife and baby son? A person who could accept that he was a man and move on?

Caris, a strange heaviness and a strange lightness in her chest, turned to George. She threw her arms around him. "You did it. It's perfect. Congratulations."

*****

Shirley and Lena emerged from the bathroom a few minutes later, Shirley's eyes red and puffy. The realism of the picture, and the hope contained therein, had apparently sent Shirley off in tears. Caris noticed that Shirley went up to George, clutched his hand, and kissed his cheek. Maybe Shirley and George would find their way back together.

Caris ventured a look at Lena, too, for as long as was appropriate. Lena.

Lena.

Her hair was short, shoulder length. She was lovelier than before. Lena gave Caris a soft smile. A fearful, nervous smile. The look was so galvanizing it sent a tremor through Caris. Lena loved her, plain and simple.

Caris became aware Shirley and George were watching. She smoothed her shirt and proffered a grin. "Hi, Shirley."

"Caris." Shirley attempted a smile and bestowed a real one upon Donovan. "He's gotten big."

"Yes," Caris said. "He has."

Caris and Lena went to the beginning of the series of drawings. The first one was titled *Birth* and showed a baby in the arms of its mother. Caris recognized the mother as a younger Shirley. So this was Dale as a baby.

"He's so good," Caris murmured.

"He's done Mom's entire life, hasn't he?" Lena's tones were awed.

"Looks like it."

"You smell good," Lena said.

"So do you."

Lena laughed. "I'm not wearing perfume."

"You smell good anyway." *Must be pheromones.* "How is Aron?"

"She's good. She enjoyed meeting you. A lot."

"I enjoyed meeting her, too. How's work? School?"

"Good. Good. How's your stuff?"

"Good. Great." *Enough of this small talk.* Caris wanted to slip her hand in Lena's, tell Lena she loved her, and kiss Lena forever and ever. No romantic interlude happened. Instead, Lena and Caris saw Dale as a teenager, Dale at her first wedding, Dale and Reggie with their baby daughter, Dale in the hospital bed with sickly Reggie, Dale kneeling at Reggie's grave, Dale marrying Caris, Dale in the hospital after the wreck, Shirley reading Agatha to Dale, Dale at Pinewood (titled *Hibernation*) and then, of course, the glorious *Spring*.

Dale grinning widely. Dale holding Donovan. Dale in physical therapy. Dale walking with the help of a cane. Dale with stubble, with a slightly older Lena and two beautiful dark-skinned young adults in purple graduation gowns. Dale with white hair, more stubble, a full beard, at Donovan's graduation — with Caris.

The last drawing was titled *Happy at Ninety*, and showed an old man, Dale, in a wheelchair, surrounded by his family — Caris, Donovan, Lena, Reggie, Aron, Nakeem and even Shirley and George, who would be long dead by then.

Oh my God, Caris thought. *What a finale.*

"What is this?" Shirley demanded. "Why does my daughter have a beard in —" she counted — "six drawings?"

"I didn't know you were coming," George whispered. "You said you didn't want to leave her."

"George. What is —"

"I would've told you if I'd known you were coming. I didn't mean you to find out like this."

"Mom is transgender," Lena said. "Transgender."

Chapter 22

George's drawings gave Lena nightmares for the next couple of weeks. Oh, not nightmares in the traditional sense, but nightmares as in unsettling, haunting dreams. The nightmares started like this:

Lena awoke one morning, Caris in her arms. Lena checked the time. Five-thirty. An uneasy sensation gnawed at her stomach. The urge to look at Caris, to make sure she was still there, that she was all right and okay, seized Lena. Darkness reigned outside. Caris was barely visible, so Lena reached over Caris and turned the lamp on. Lena kept her breathing and movements to a minimum, content to study Caris's profile. Her lips were slightly parted, and drool trickled a slick path down her jaw. Her hair was a rainbow on her pillow. "You're beautiful," Lena murmured, love for Caris burning her body. "I hope I make you as happy as you make me."

Ring. Caris's cell, not Lena's. Caris never turned her phone off. Lena had never asked why. No need to. You never knew when there would be news.

Ring.

The gnawing at Lena's stomach became more insistent, and a heaviness settled in her heart. She felt in her gut the reason for the call. *It's here. It's time.* The day of reckoning. Her mother was gone. Lena wondered what the culprit had been. Blood clots were tricky, hard to detect. Or maybe it had been a stroke. A hemorrhage. An infection gone bad.

Caris did not stir.

Ring.

Funny. The split second between each ring felt like a month.

Quit stalling. Answer the damn thing already.

Lena reached over Caris and grabbed the phone, disconnecting it from the charger. "Hello?" Lena sat naked, cross legged, her muscles tense and waiting.

A surprised breath. A rich voice with deep timbers. "Hello. This is Dr. Aronson. I need to speak to Caris."

"She's—" Lena rubbed Caris's shoulder gently. "Caris? She's sleeping. This is Lena. Tell me what happened. It's better if the news comes from me, anyway."

"It's incredible, Lena. Your mother's awake."

Lena swallowed hard. "Was it peaceful?" Her mother must have been alone. Shirley would not be there this early. *No one should have to die alone.*

"She's awake. Awake!"

Dr. Aronson's words finally penetrated. "Awake?"

"Awake. She opened her eyes not even fifteen minutes ago and said: 'Lena?' "

"What?"

"She's awake!"

Lena's pulse wobbled. Her brain shivered. *Awake. No way.* "You mean she's gone. She's dead."

"She's awake and talking. I'm at home but I'm going right in to Pinewood after I call Shirley. Later today, we'll transfer your mother to Inova Fairfax for tests." Dr. Aronson said something else, but the bedroom spun around Lena. *Wait. I'm dreaming. That's what this is.* She was sleeping. Lena looked around the room, which continued to be topsy-turvy. She focused on a framed photo of Caris and Donovan. The room slowly stabilized.

"Hello?"

Lena fought through her cobwebs. "What?"

"Wake your stepmother up and tell her. She needs to get here as soon as possible. You, too."

"Yes. But wait, Dr. Aronson. She's awake? Mom's awake?"

"I have to get going. Tell Caris to come in, okay? As soon as possible. We don't know how long your mother will be alert."

"Bye." Lena hung up. Five minutes passed.

"Uhmm." Caris was waking up now. Her eyes flickered open, and Lena got a glimpse of lovely blue. She decided to stay quiet about the phone call. For a minute, anyway. She would enjoy what she had while it lasted, before the past thundered down on them.

Caris smiled, a pure I-love-you smile. "Last night was great," she said. Lena saw nothing of the past in Caris's expression. She saw only joy, happiness, love. A future. Lena's throat knotted. She tried to brush the phone call away, pretend it didn't exist. Such a task was impossible. She began with a stumble, aware that she was being too blunt, too rough, but was not sure how to give the news the padding and careful handling it required. "Dr. Aronson called. Mom is awake."

Caris jerked like she had sat on a bed of knives. "What?"

Lena got out of bed. "Get to Pinewood as soon as possible."

And then Shirley walked into the bedroom. "She'll be okay," Shirley said. "I'll pray. God will make sure she's okay. She'll be moving around in no time. Stem cells are amazing things. She'll be walking around in no time, I guarantee."

"She won't be okay!" Lena exclaimed. "What kind of life will she have if her brain's okay but she can't move? If she can't go to the bathroom by herself?"

"That's not your decision. I'll make sure she has the sex change surgery. We'll get her in shape for that. You must think positive, Lena. You must."

*****

In reality, Dale died the day after Christmas. The phone rang, Lena saw who the caller was, and her gut told her why Shirley was calling.

"Your mother died," Shirley said, without preamble.

Lena was at home and had been debating whether to stop by the townhouse to drop off a Christmas present for Donovan, a present Lena had bought in October. Lena had a gift for Caris too, but she had decided to not give it, only Donovan's. *Your mother died. Your mother died.* The pain of the words was immense, searing, wriggling into Lena's empty spaces, filling her. Lena felt faint, and she pinched her arm. *Feel later. Mourn later.* "Okay, Grandma. Okay. Please don't call Caris. I'll go tell her right now, and then I'll meet you at Pinewood."

*****

As Lena waited for Caris to answer the doorbell, she thought: *Funny how things come full circle.* She had been the one to tell Caris about the car accident; Caris had thought Dale was dead. And now Caris would get that final news. Donovan's present was in the car. Best to deliver the news right away, to not let Caris get comfortable and think the call was social.

Jennifer answered the door. "Lena," she said none too enthusiastically.

"Hey, Jennifer. Is Caris in?" Lena tried to smile. She had nothing against Caris's best friend, but Jennifer had never liked her. No wonder, given the fact Lena had not bothered to get to know Caris after Dale announced the engagement. And if Jennifer knew about her and Caris...probably another reason not to like Lena.

"We're having lunch," Jennifer said.

"I won't be long."

Jennifer held the door open, and Lena made her way into the living room. Caris had gone light on Christmas decorations, which was no surprise. Dale had never been big on holidays, and Lena's own apartment had no decorations. Here, a tree stood in a corner, a few wrapped presents scattered under it. Lena wondered if one was for her.

"Are you here about your mother?" Jennifer asked.

"It's that obvious?"

———

143

Jennifer quirked her eyebrows. "Did..."

Is she dead? Did she kick the bucket? Did she bite the dust? Is that what you mean? "Yes," Lena said.

"Oh, Lena." Jennifer touched her hand to Lena's shoulder. "I'm sorry."

"Me too. Thank you."

"How did she go?"

"My grandmother didn't say. I'm going to Pinewood after I tell Caris."

"I'll tell her."

Lena squeezed her fists. *I want to tell her. I'm her lover. Or should be. I'm the woman she loves.* She could not voice her protestations, though. Caris's wife was dead. This was not the time for territorial squabbling. Jennifer was as good a person as any to break the news.

Lena followed Jennifer into the dining room. "Look who's here," Jennifer called.

A smile lit up Caris's face. Her hair was in a ponytail, and she was feeding Donovan in his high chair. "Lena! Hey. Perfect timing. Donovan was saying we needed to give you your Christmas present."

"He did, huh? That's a bright eight-month-old."

"You weren't speaking in full sentences at eight months?"

"I don't think I've mastered full sentences yet." Lena had meant the comment teasingly, but her voice sounded solemn and stern.

"What's wrong?" Caris asked, and Jennifer went to her.

Lena continued standing where she was, on the periphery of the dining room, and forced her gaze to the microwave. Lena did not want to intrude on the private moment, and all she could hear was Shirley's voice: *Your mother died. Your mother died. Your mother died. Your mother died.*

Lena hoped Jennifer knew how to tell Caris right.

*****

"She was the same as usual," Shirley said numbly. "I went to the bathroom, refilled my water bottle and got peanut M&Ms. When I got back, Dale was slumped over and cold."

Lena stole a glance at Caris. She was pale. Dale remained in the wheelchair; probably Shirley or an orderly had straightened her. Her eyes were closed, no grimaces, no frowns, nothing, but she did not particularly look at peace. Just some indefinable thing. Lena did not voice her thought. Probably *she* was the one not at peace. "Mom looks so small," Lena said.

Shirley wiped at her eyes with a tissue. "At least she didn't die in bed. Or in a gown. She wouldn't want that."

"Yes, thank you," Caris said mechanically. "For getting her dressed this morning."

"You know what Lena said when I called her?"

Huh? Lena risked a look at her grandmother. What was Shirley getting at?

"No," Caris replied softly.

"Lena didn't ask how it happened, how her own mother died. All she said was: 'Okay, Grandma. Okay. Please don't call Caris. I'll tell her right now, and I'll meet you at Pinewood.' And Lena's voice was flat. No emotion."

Caris's eyelashes fluttered. "Oh."

"Lena's first thought was about *you*. Not about her own mother."

Awesome, Grandma. Awesome. "Grandma, I'd been expecting this for a while. You knew it had to be coming too."

Shirley swiveled her gaze to Lena. "She's your mother's wife!"

"You don't know what's going on in my head, okay? So don't pretend you do. Caris is—she has—she's not a monster. You think we jumped into bed for the hell of it? I wouldn't do something like that to my mother. Caris and I—"

"Do you love her?" Shirley asked the question with a mixture of curiosity, bitterness and distaste.

"Do I love..." *Oh, geez.* Lena had no intention of declaring her love to Caris this way. "I love you, Grandma, and we'll talk about this later."

Shirley's lips set in a thin line, but she assented with a nod. She tore open her package of peanut M&Ms. After a moment's hesitation, she proffered the bag to Lena. Lena took a few of the candies, and then Shirley offered the bag to Caris.

"Thank you, Shirley," Caris said. She took a few M&Ms.

The three of them munched in silence until one of the orderlies stuck his head in. "Excuse me. Mr. Vincent and Mr. Thomas from the funeral home are here."

Shirley got to her feet. "I'll talk to them."

Lena rose as well. "I'll go with you." *Give Caris alone time with Mom.* Lena was under the impression that Caris had not visited Dale in quite some time.

When Lena returned five minutes later, Caris seemed to not have moved. Lena took Caris's hand and kissed it. "Are you ready for them to take the body away?"

Caris grimaced. "Body. Do you want a few minutes with—"

"No. I had a good time with her yesterday. She smiled. I really think she did. That's what I want our last time together to be."

Chapter 23

"We chose a mahogany red casket," Caris said at the townhouse that night. She showed George a picture.

"Nice."

Truth be told, Caris barely remembered her, Shirley and Lena picking out the casket. She barely remembered them making the arrangements. Caris had not realized things would move this fast. Dale was so freshly dead, and here they were making arrangements.

They could have waited until tomorrow, probably. But Shirley needed something to do. Something to channel her anxiety, her nervous energy, into. The three of them had mostly spoken to other people. Not to one another.

"I'm going to be cremated," Caris said. The statement was directed toward no one in particular, although George was closest. He was next to her on the couch, Shirley was in the kitchen with a couple of neighbors heating up a casserole for dinner, Jennifer was feeding Donovan in a chair across the room, and Lena was standing by the front windows, her arms crossed.

Caris wanted all these people to go away. Except Lena. No second chance for Dale. No *Spring*.

I'm so sorry, Dale.

Lena smiled slightly. "I want to be cryogenically frozen."

"What's that?" Jennifer asked.

"Your body is frozen. When the technology's there, you're revived. Say cancer killed you. When you're revived in the future, cancer is no problem. Easy peasy."

"Are you serious?"

Lena shrugged. "Why not? If it doesn't work, I won't know. The world is a wonderful place. I want to be around to see it five hundred years from now. A thousand."

Jennifer snorted. "You're kidding, right? That's not going to work."

Lena shot her a glare. "Like I said. If it doesn't work, I won't know."

Shirley and the neighbors came back with the food, but Caris brushed her offering off.

"Cryonics," George mused. "That's the Ted Williams thing. Didn't something happen with his head?"

"Maybe some cracks in it," Lena said.

Caris tuned out the conversation. Part of her, deep down inside, had thought Dale would get a second chance. She heard a few snatches here and there: *John Henry Williams, leukemia, will, cremated, Alcor, tuna can...*

Absurd.

Being frozen would not be too bad. She would set Jennifer straight. Tell Jennifer to show Lena respect. Caris and Lena could experience the future together. Five hundred years from now, no one would know their history, that Caris used to be Lena's stepmother. No gossip, whispered glances behind their backs. *Oh my gosh, her wife was barely in the hospital before she hopped in bed with her stepdaughter.* No people wondering if they'd been carrying on an affair before Dale's wreck.

Frozen. Clean start.

Caris's shoulders ached. Her chest ached. Her arms ached. The rain in Paris for their honeymoon had been wet, gleeful. Dale had been like a child, laughing and stepping in puddles. Why the hell not? They were drenched already and hopelessly lost.

At Snowshoe, in West Virginia, Caris could not get the hang of skiing. She fell every time she dismounted the lifts. Dale was patient and helped Caris up every time, explained what she needed to do.

Wasn't the same Dale in the wheelchair. Dead, pathetic, lonely Dale.

Caris excused herself, saying she had to go to the bathroom. Instead, she headed to her bedroom. She got a blue envelope and slipped the rings inside. Then she wrote a letter.

Dear Dale,

I've been thinking. That night I was in the bathtub and you visited wasn't a dream, was it? It was your way of communicating with me in that hazy land between consciousness and unconsciousness, between sleep and wakefulness. I still feel the touch of you, of your face, from that night. Your skin was smooth, just a teeny bit oily. You were there. Period.

Like Dr. Aronson says, consciousness is tricky.

I'm glad we got that last time together. Thank you. I hope you're with Reggie now and that you two are happy.

I love you.

-Caris

The evening dragged on and on. Neighbors and a few of Dale's co-workers were in and out. Caris stayed away from Lena. Lena stayed away from her. What else could they do?

At last, though, only Jennifer and Lena remained. Caris checked the time. Eleven o'clock.

"You look tired," Jennifer said to Caris.

"I am."

"I'll stay tonight and take care of Donovan."

"Go home. I'm fine. You've done more than enough. You rest."

"You haven't eaten."

"Haven't been hungry."

Lena got up from the couch. She stretched, her body long and limber like a cat's. The picture of casualness. Caris did not want Lena to be this good at acting. Did not want herself to be this good, either.

"See you guys tomorrow," Lena said.

Caris's thoughts scampered. No way about it. "Will you stay tonight?"

Lena's lips tugged up. She nodded.

Jennifer frowned. "I said I'll stay."

Lena patted Jennifer's shoulder. "Thank you, but I got this."

Jennifer shrugged off the touch. "You don't even like your stepmother."

"I said I got this," Lena repeated, an edge in her voice. "Caris wants me to stay, so I'm staying. I'll heat up food. We'll eat. It's all right, I promise. I will take care of her."

Caris could not help but smile. *I will take care of her.* Caris hoped Lena would let Caris take care of her, too. Lena had seemed lost all day. Lost and wooden and detached. They had both been putting on brave faces. Maybe now they could be themselves.

A dismayed, understanding look crossed Jennifer's features. She met Caris's gaze. "Her?"

"What's wrong with her?"

Jennifer got her purse and left without saying goodbye.

*****

"I'm cold," Lena said, and she was glad when Caris put her arms around her.

"Want soup?" Caris asked.

"No."

"My first night home after having Donovan, I took a bath. Bubble bath. I kept waiting for the hospital to call that your mother was dead."

"Want to take a bath together?"

"I would love to. Hey, are you holding up okay?"

"No," Lena said. "Not really. My mother is dead."

"Part of me thought—hoped—she'd wake up and get her second chance. Especially after what your grandfather did."

"I guess part of me did, too. Maybe it wasn't a cry for help. Maybe she actually meant to kill herself."

Caris sighed, looking impossibly weary. "Maybe she did."

Caris got into the bathtub first, and Lena rested her head against

Caris's chest. She was content to let Caris hold her. Content to listen to Caris's heartbeat. Caris's heat and the water were exactly what Lena needed, and she felt most of her worries drift away. "I have a Christmas present for Donovan in my car," she whispered.

"What is it?"

"Cute little bowling shoes. I didn't know what else to get him. He probably can't use the shoes for a few years, but..."

Caris groaned. "You're gonna teach him to kick my ass."

Lena laughed. "Yep. And better sooner rather than later. I also got you — I wasn't going to give them to you because of — well, it doesn't matter. I got you bowling shoes, too. Pretty shoes. They're white. They look more like tennis shoes than bowling shoes."

"Thank you, Lena," Caris murmured. "The three of us going bowling. That would be nice."

"Yes."

"I'm sorry about Jennifer," Caris said.

"She doesn't like me."

"She didn't like how you used to cancel on me all the time. She'll come around. I'll talk to her. We didn't break the news in the best way."

Lena maneuvered around. *Splosh splosh splosh.* She faced Caris. "I don't want to make the same mistake Mom did."

"Okay."

"She couldn't be honest with you, the woman she loved, because she feared losing you. I want to be honest with you."

"I want to be honest with you, too."

Lena's heart fluttered, and she took one last look at Caris. One last look before everything would change, whether for the better or the worse. Lena kissed Caris, first on her left cheek, then her right, then on her mouth. The kiss was much like their first kiss, passionate and intense and sad and eager and playful and solemn all at the same time, and electrifying every part of Lena, especially her heart.

This time, it was Lena, not Caris, who ended the kiss. "You're different," Lena said. "I can't explain how, but you are. A relationship is what the people in it make it to be. You can spread your wings. I don't want to clip your wings, not at all. Date people and live your life. When you're ready, if you want me, you — we can — something like that. And screw Grandma. She'll come around eventually. She already is. She let you have some of her M&Ms."

Caris laughed, and Lena kept going. "If I did not feel what I feel for you and for Donovan, I would not be involved with you like I am. I had two babies, I let them go, and I have to watch from a distance as they grow and live their lives. I'm not their mother in the way that counts, and that probably *is* for the best because they have wonderful parents. But I don't want to watch Donovan grow up from a distance. If I thought for one second I was not right for you or Donovan, that I could not help you or make you happy, I would let go so you could find someone else. On paper, we don't look like we fit. But in real life, we do. That's what I think. We have to try. I love you, Caris. I've loved you a long time."

Caris took Lena in her arms, and Lena held onto Caris's slick, soapy body. "I love you, Lena. I love you very much. We will be fine. I don't care about dating other people. You're the one."

Lena blinked back tears. She was going to cry. Now. She did not want to, of course not, not in front of Caris. Caris had been right. It was the limbo, why Lena had not been able to cry. However, Lena could do nothing, could not even move, because all of a sudden she was crying. Hard. Too hard. Crying like she never had before. She was crying because she was at peace, she had confessed she loved Caris, she was crying because of Nakeem Joseph, who did not like her, and for Aron Michelle, who let Lena be her kind of stepmother, and for Joanna's forgiveness, and for George and his drawings, and for Shirley, who ached for her daughter, and whose leaving at the wrong time meant Dale died alone, and crying in gratefulness that Shirley shared her M&Ms with Caris, because that meant Shirley was going to try to accept them together. Lena also cried for Caris and for Donovan, Donovan who was going to be her baby too. Lena cried for all the families waiting, all the families still in limbo, and for her own lost, misguided mannequin of a mother who had grabbed fairy dust and was a person again in wherever place she—he—was now.

*****

Afterward, Caris led her to bed. They burrowed under the sheets, their arms and legs entangled, two as one. For the first time, they kissed without limitation, without hurry, without fear. "I love you," Caris said, and Lena said: "I love you, too."

"It's ironic, you know," Caris said. "We're going to be like your mother."

"What do you mean?"

"If we're cryogenically frozen. We'll be in limbo."

"I hadn't thought of it that way. You're right."

Caris drifted off to sleep, and Lena imagined their future together. Five hundred years from now, maybe they would have another awakening. They would wake up in a different time and a different place, but they would be together. Always.

*****

About a month after Dale's death, George moved back to Virginia. He and Shirley were reconciling. He invited Caris, Lena and Donovan over for the unveiling of his latest drawing. "It's titled *Where the Wind Goes*," he said, and unveiled it.

Dale was on the boat. George had finally gotten the scene right. Caris could taste the salt water and feel the wind whipping Dale's hair. She could reach out, touch Dale's chapped cheeks and hear Dale's brilliant, gusty laughter.

"That's her," Shirley said. "Him, I mean. Him. Dale is happy."

*****

A few evenings later, Lena and Aron stopped by the townhouse for a visit. Aron was spending the night with Lena again and brought an Agatha Christie book to read to Donovan. Caris and Lena worked on a brain teaser game together while Aron read.

"The watcher's post was empty," Aron read. "Jimmy Thesiger was not there. Bundle stared in complete amazement. What had happened? Why had Jimmy left his post? What did it mean?"

Donovan laughed.

"What do you think happened?" Aron asked the baby.

"La mo!"

Aron had met Donovan a few times and was in love with the child. She'd always wanted a little brother or sister. Now she had one. Caris could not help but remember one of her thoughts soon after Donovan's birth: *The baby will need his big sister.* Donovan had a big sister after all, just not Lena.

"I think Jimmy was there," Caris said. "But he had turned into a bug. Therefore, Jimmy was so tiny Bundle could not see him."

Aron giggled. "What kind of bug?"

"Ladybug?"

"Oooh. I love ladybugs. They're pretty. Hey, Caris. Are you and Lena gonna get married someday?"

Caris could not help but smile. She directed her gaze to Lena and cocked an eyebrow.

"I...I..." Lena's cheeks had turned pink. "Yes, I think so." She closed her hand over Caris's. "Yes, we will. Definitely."

THE END

Notable patients who are or were
in persistent vegetative or minimally conscious states

Comas have many causes, including brain trauma and hemorrhage. In cases of traumatic brain injury, doctors will sometimes order a reversible drug-induced coma to give the brain time to heal. Most people remain in comas for a few days to a few weeks, although in exceptional cases, a coma may last years. The prognosis for coma patients runs the gamut from recovery to death. Two of the outcomes for coma patients are emergence into a minimally conscious state or a persistent vegetative state. Patients in minimally conscious states exhibit erratic and rare periods of true responsiveness. As many as forty percent of people in persistent vegetative states may be misdiagnosed and actually are minimally conscious. Vegetative state patients have no awareness whatsoever. What follows is a list of notable people who emerged from a coma into one these two states.

Patient file # 1: ·
Esposito, Elaine (1934-1978) was six years old when she went into the hospital for a regular appendectomy. She never woke up from the anesthetic. She fell into a persistent vegetative state and remained in it for thirty-seven years, one hundred and eleven days, setting a Guinness World Record.

Patient file # 2:
Quinlan, Karen Ann (1954-1985) was twenty-one when came she home from a party and fell unconscious from alcohol and drugs. Her breathing stopped for at least fifteen minutes on two occasions. She was on a ventilator, in a persistent vegetative state, and did not improve, so her family requested the hospital disconnect the ventilator. Faced with threats by the Morris County, New Jersey, prosecutor to bring homicide charges against them, the hospital officials refused . The family eventually prevailed through the legal system, and in 1976, the hospital disconnected Karen Quinlan's ventilator. However, she stunned her family and officials by continuing to breathe on her own. She stayed in the persistent vegetative state until she died from pneumonia in 1985.

Patient file # 3:

Cruzan, Nancy Beth (1957-1990) swerved off the road in January 1983. She was driving a car without seat belts and landed face down in a water-filled ditch. She did not breathe for fifteen minutes, but somehow, paramedics resuscitated her. She was in a coma for a couple of weeks and emerged into a persistent vegetative state. Her family worked untiringly for five years to improve her condition, to bring her back to consciousness, but eventually petitioned all the way to the U.S. Supreme Court for the right to pull Cruzan's feeding tube. The Supreme Court denied the motion, saying there was a lack of evidence of what Cruzan would have wanted. On December 14, 1990, a Missouri circuit court ruled that new evidence presented by three more friends constituted "clear and convincing" evidence Nancy Cruzan would not want to continue existing in a persistent vegetative state and allowed the removal of her artificial feeding tube. Nancy Cruzan died twelve days after the removal of her feeding tube.

Patient file #4:

Bland, Anthony David "Tony" (1970-1993) was one of the soccer fans crushed during the Hillsborough Disaster, a stampede of fans during a Liverpool soccer game. He had two punctured lungs, causing irreversible brain damage due to lack of oxygen to his brain. Left in a persistent vegetative state, he was the first person the British courts allowed to die through removal of life-prolonging means.

Patient file #5:

Dockery, Gary French (1954-1997) was a police officer shot in the forehead in 1988. He lapsed into a persistent vegetative state. Seven and a half years later, fluid was filling his lungs, and his family agonized over what to do: operate or let him go. They opted for lung surgery, and on February 11, 1996, shortly after the operation, Dockery suddenly awoke and began to chatter nonstop. He remembered the names of family and friends, his pets, details of camping trips and the color of his car. Some doctors speculated he had been in a minimally conscious state, not a persistent vegetative state. Whatever his true condition had been, he fell silent again after 18 hours. He died on April 15, 1997, from a blood clot in his lung.

Patient file #6:

Schiavo, Theresa Marie "Terri" (1963-2005) fell victim to cardio-respiratory arrest (causes unclear) in 1990. She was in a persistent vegetative state for fifteen years. Her husband and her parents waged a fierce legal battle with each other, with her husband claiming she would not have wanted the life-prolonging support. Michael Schiavo's efforts eventually succeeded, and Terri Schiavo died after thirteen days without her feeding tube.

Patient file #7:
Von Bulow, Sunny (1932-2008) was an heiress and socialite who fell into a persistent vegetative state (causes unclear) in 1980. She stayed in it for almost twenty-eight years, until she died in a nursing home.

Patient file #8:
Englaro, Eluana (1970-2009) was an Italian woman in a persistent vegetative state for seventeen years after a car accident. She became the intense focus of a battle between supporters and opponents of euthanasia, dubbed Italy's "Terri Schiavo." Her father fought a decade-long legal battle to let his daughter die, per what he argued were her wishes. He and her friends testified in court, giving evidence she would not have wanted to artificially prolong her life. She died four days after the removal of life support.

Patient file #9:
Cheng, Chi (1970- alive as of October 2011) was the bassist in the American rock band Deftones. He was in a car accident in 2008 and remains in a minimally conscious state. He tracks people with his eyes, sometimes can make responses with words, and can purposefully, although slightly, move his hands.

Patient file #10:
Wallis, Terry (1964-alive as of October 2011) spent almost twenty years in a minimally conscious state before regaining awareness. In 2003, unexpectedly, he began to speak. He still lives with disabilities produced by the automobile accident that caused his condition and continues to receive extensive speech and physical therapy.

Patient file #11:
Sharon, Ariel (1928-alive as of October 2011) was Israel's eleventh prime minister. He suffered a massive stroke on January 4, 2006, and remains in a persistent vegetative state. He has survived despite severe kidney and lung problems. As of 2010, the formally robust, 255-pound Ariel Sharon weighed 110 pounds.

CHECK OUT Q. KELLY'S OTHER BOOKS,
AVAILABLE IN E-BOOK AND PAPERBACK

Strange Bedfellows: What happens when the queen of the ex-gay movement decides to come out of the closet? The person who helps Frances Dourne with this enormous task is a call girl Frances hires. A call girl with a secret of her own. Can they learn to trust each other enough to find the love they seek in each other's arms?

Frances is grappling with something else, too. Her daughter, Marissa, has been gone 11 years. She was kidnapped by her father on her third birthday. Frances hopes her coming out will ease the way for Marissa's return.

*****

The Odd Couple: Morrisey Hawthorne and her four-year-old son, Gareth, have a pretty good life. Then one day they meet Charlene Sudsbury, who is trying to move on from the suicide of her son, JP, three years before. Gareth is nearly the mirror image of JP, and Charlene connects instantly with him. Not quite so with Morrisey, who can't escape fast enough after Charlene shows her a picture of JP. Charlene is convinced Morrisey is hiding something and sets out in search of the truth.

Despite the circumstances, the two women form an unusual bond and end up with a lot more than they bargained for. But when an old friend of JP's resurfaces, he challenges the fragile trust Morrisey and Charlene have been building.

Can these two women overcome the obstacles that separate them from the happiness they seek?

Check Q. Kelly out at http://qkelly.blogspot.com
and at http://qkelly.wordpress.com

Email her at yllek_q@yahoo.com

17088473R00083

Made in the USA
Lexington, KY
28 August 2012